Love in One Night

A Real Negus Novella

Dandridge Monroe

ISBN:
ISBN-13:

To the one who forced me to believe in true love, no matter how quickly it happens, you are still M1AO

For my sisters, my biggest cheerleaders and supporters, I love y'all.

The KMKs, you are both still the beats of my heart.

To my angel—I love you always.

CHAPTER ONE

Her

Hour Zero

I can't believe I'm doing this.

One of my dark honey brown hands twirled a tube of mascara as I stood in front of the mirror contemplating the shit I was about to get myself into.

And it was some heavy shit.

Like some *keep me out of heaven* shit.

Some *bald-headed ho* shit.

Well, some high dollar bald-headed ho shit. So, some escort shit?

Even my conscience was calling me a hooker. But by the way I was still going through the motions of getting dressed and packed for this...event, my ass was obviously not that concerned.

Beats being alone, right?

No one wanted to spend the most romantic day of the year by themselves, especially when it was the first time in years you'd had to.

Even with a ouija board, crystal ball, and tarot cards, I never would've seen any of this coming.

My life had been on hold for a few months since the tragedy struck. And that was literally the only word to describe the bullshit that had unfolded just before Thanksgiving. My view on holidays was permanently fucked up and I had to make this one memorable in some capacity so that I didn't go on strike and hate them all and turn into a Scrooge. My mom already called me a Grinch at Christmas and I hated that one person had so much control over my attitude. That was too much like letting evil win.

In less than week I needed to take the first step into the rest of my life and this weekend would allow me to do so. I just never thought I'd be taking this step by my damn self.

My entire life was legit depending on one night.

I couldn't sell sex, confidence, and strength when I lacked those things myself. You could only fake the funk so long before the lies began to erode your soul. Since my entire life was built on authenticity, there was no way I could claim this next positive achievement without releasing the negative in me.

And this was one hell of a way to release that negative.

Lord, if you're watching, close your eyes for about fifteen hours.

I dropped the mascara wand, glanced into the mirror and noted that, for the first time in months, my eyes were no longer weary. The dark brown orbs gleamed and the bags that were once my constant companions were fading away. My skin seemed to shine more from within than from the facial I'd indulged in this morning and I looked less...destroyed.

Heartbroken.

Gutted.

Those adjectives had been my constant companions hanging around like that Zoloft cloud over my head. But it looked like maybe the sun was breaking through on its own and it was merely from the *anticipation* of what was to come.

If I had the ability to reconnect with myself the way I wanted to after this...excursion...I'd be looking like my old self in no time.

Better than my old self even.

So yeah, the scalleywag behavior was still on go.

With a smile gracing my full lips, I continued to study my reflection.

The only thing that felt off was the hair helmet I'd allowed my friend Sasha to convince me to try. I'd done it on a whim and though she didn't know the reasons why I wanted the change she offered her advice anyway.

Perks of being friends with a supermodel.

I could admit that it looked real as hell, but the color was what was throwing me off. I'd never been so...adventurous with my look, but anonymity was a must right about now. The upcoming changes in my professional life would eventually have my brand, and therefore my face, plastered on billboards and in magazines. I doubt my mother would recognize me right now. The dark roots of the *hairmet* gave way to an almost ash gray color that looked surprisingly beautiful next to my skin. The goal was to be less recognizable and this wig and makeup job was doing the trick. At least I didn't look like I'd snatched Barbie's wig and glued it to my forehead.

I left the bathroom and entered my closet looking for the pair of red stilettos that would set off my entire outfit. My eyes strayed to the garment bag that was shoved in the back of the closet. The entire room was built to look like a high-end boutique with white lacquered cabinetry and a modern center island topped in quartz and the dark black bag stuck out like a whore in church.

Feeling the bile that wanted to rise as always when I saw that bag, I pulled out my phone and called the only person who would be able to talk me off this cliff—my mama. Common sense would have said to get rid of it, but there was something that kept that shit hanging there. Maybe as a reminder of my stupidity. A monument to my failures that I could revisit to keep me humble? A monument to what happened when you played yourself. Whatever it was, I didn't need to see it right now.

Waiting for the line to connect, I exhaled a frustrated breath and willed the tears that wanted to form to stay their asses where they were. I wasn't about to have to explain to my ophthalmologist yet again that I'd cried too hard and ruptured a vessel. Now that was some weak bitch shit I wouldn't ever forget.

"Nev, what are you doing calling me tonight? You know me and your daddy were about to get into some thangs."

My face balled up immediately and that bile that I thought she would keep contained was threatening to spew all over this expensive ass white carpet. Those tears of sadness threatened to turn into disgust at her words.

"Ma, nobody wants to hear about whatever geriatric gymnastics you and my daddy are trying to get into. I called because I need a favor." I held my breath because I knew her psychic ass knew what was up and was about to talk major shit.

She huffed then started to chuckle and I contained my huff of indignation because I didn't want to hear the *I told you so* that was about to come out of her mouth.

"So you finally decided to stop listening to the bullshit that troll-faced bastard you called a *fiancé* was trying to spit? Want to find himself after he got us spending money on a wedding. I hope you've burned all his shit. And trust me that dress is going in the trash. We don't need that kind of bad juju hanging around your house."

See, there it was.

I sighed and looked at the emptied out half of a closet that was custom built to accommodate two people whose livelihoods depended on how well they presented themselves to the public. I was grateful that this entire debacle happened before I made this next step. Otherwise, I would've had so much more to deal with.

Look at me, being happy about something that came out of this bullshit. This was progress indeed.

Grabbing the shoes that I initially went in there for, I went back to continue packing.

"I know, Ma. You told me to leave him alone. You said he was sneaky, I should've listened." I put the shoes in their dust covers and zipped them up in my carryon. It was no secret that she'd never liked my ex. Hell, truth be told, it took a lot for me to agree to go out with him in the first place. But what I thought was Black love and building was really failures and fallacies wrapped up in immaculate game and tied with a Purple Label bow. You lived and you learned; and sometimes those lessons damn near cost you your sanity.

She sucked her teeth and I could damn near hear her roll her eyes over the phone. "Don't make me break your daddy's heart and come over there to beat your ass, little girl. You ain't too grown for me to make you pick a switch."

She had me fucked up, but I knew better than to say anything.

"Ma, I am admitting that you're right. Isn't that what all mothers dream of?" I was laying it on thick, but I had a flight to catch and an ego to jumpstart. I had gotten her to agree to detoxifying my house, so she could get back to the *geriatric ho shit* her and my daddy were about to be on. Hopefully she would sage this motherfucker too or else I would finally take her advice and put it on the market.

She clucked her tongue which was an indication she was about to say something smart.

"Don't think I don't know you're rushing me off this phone. I'm going to hope to God and the deities your daddy's people still follow that you're rushing me off the phone because you have somewhere to be. As long as it ain't with that sneaky bastard you have my blessing."

See, psychic. She knew exactly what the hell she was doing when she said that. She knew my ass was up to something and that I wouldn't tell her what. Even though she normally found out anyway. I didn't want her pity or for her to talk me out of doing this. She would make far too much sense and have me questioning whether or not my brain chemistry had been severely altered by this tragedy. That or I had fallen and bumped my head. Either way, she would probably send someone here to stage an intervention and have Iyanla here in the flesh to speak to me about better decision making skills and the need to not self-harm by indulging in risky behaviors. She could really be extra sometimes.

"As long as you're not going to question me I'm good. And to put you at ease, I'm not going anywhere near the sneaky bastard so rest easy and get back to doing whatever it was you had planned. And no, I don't need to know what it was." Zipping up the carryon my eyes darted around the room to ensure I hadn't forgotten anything.

"Whatever you're about to do, Nev, have fun. I miss seeing you smile, honey." Her voice had softened in that motherly way and gone was the woman who was always joking. This was her subtle way of letting me know she was worried and I couldn't help but smile at her concern. My mother was a firecracker but her mother lioness would roar whenever she felt her cubs were threatened. This was a shock to us all and I was sure she was working herself into a fit because she didn't have the answers for me. And even if she did, I wouldn't want them. This was time for me to be the overcomer and save myself. My methods were unconventional, but something inside told me this was the best route to shake off the last vestiges of grief.

"I hear you mama, loud and clear. Kiss my daddy for me," I heard her cackle and I had to add a caveat to that statement, "on the cheek mama! Kiss him on the cheek for me!" Lord only knows where her mind went.

"You messing up my night, Nev. When do you get back so that I can ensure that I handle this for you?"

"I'll be back on Sunday." I was only acting up for one night but would stay with my friend to 'debrief' -which was code for *was the dick any good*?- on Saturday.

"I'll get you right."

"You always do, mama. I love you."

*

After I hung up with my mother, I dialed the number to the person who got me into this…situation. I couldn't be mad at her per se, but I did feel some kind of way about being talked into doing this… prostitution shit.

"Tell me you're not backing out, Nev." Her voice was panicked and it made me want to tell her *hell yes* and then cut my phone off. Her tone was driving my anxiety about the situation into overdrive. As if there was some secret about this whole club she hadn't informed me about and her very life depended on her getting me into this hotel room. Yeah, I might have been dramatic, but shit, she needed a better poker voice.

"Tell me how you talked me into this shit again?" I flopped back on the bed as the tendrils from the *hairmet* floated around me. There was nothing interesting to look at on the ceiling but it kept my attention as I began to think of ways to back out of this.

"You need to get your sexy back and this is the perfect way to do it with no strings attached. I can't tell you who you've matched with, but you for damn sure want to get your ass here." Her near shrieking had gone from panicked to pure excitement in a matter of seconds. The change had me intrigued but I wasn't about to fly off the handle and be curious. That was the first thing I couldn't do in this situation.

"When does your flight get into Atlanta?" I could hear her clacking away on her computer as always and shuffling as she moved things around her desk. I still thought she was wasting her talent, not to mention her whole ass HBCU degrees, in her current position but she said the work was far more exciting than clinical could ever be. She never knocked my dream so I returned the favor and kept my opinions to myself.

Glancing at my smart watch I rolled my eyes and sat up. Throwing my handbag across my body I gripped the handle of my carryon.

"I'm heading to the airport now. I've got Clear so I don't have to worry about lines." My travels took me back and forth to my father's homeland of Burkina Faso, so I did everything in my power to make travel as stress free as possible. That fee was worth not having to take off my shoes, remove clothing, or wait in lines. In addition to traveling to Burkina Faso, I also did trade shows and met with buyers around the world. Since I was constantly late, I needed every advantage I could get when traveling.

She all but whined as the background noises ceased. "C'mon, Nee. Don't do this. Don't back out. I already had to kick out a chick that the boss handpicked for this dude. You legit cannot back out on me now."

See! I knew there was some shit she was holding back.

I stopped the progress I'd made to exit my house silently contemplating whether or not I was beat for this. "What?! So you know who this is?"

She gave a mischievous giggle and I could picture her sienna-colored face pulled into a sly, Grinch-like devilish grin. "If the rumors are true he is exactly what you need tonight. A charming gentleman, kinda reclusive, fine as hell and with a dick and stroke game to make bitches stalk him after a hookup. What better way to get back in the saddle than to have your pussy broken a little?"

"None of that sounds like what I need. I need someone nice who can build me up, not a nigga with a jackhammer dick trying to crack my foundation!"

"He needs to *'beat it out the frame shawty'!*" Her voice deepened and I could all but see her little bit cupping one side of her mouth as she hollered.

I shook my head at her enthusiasm even if it made me smile. "Anyone ever tell you that you're the poster child of *team too much*? Besides, this ain't *Love Connection*." I hated to even think that word in this space. The remnants of happier times played out on the large white sofa that still anchored the massive great room with the teal-colored accent wall. The argument over who got domain over decorating seemed to echo around me even though I was alone. Since my name was on the mortgage I'd won that battle but had clearly lost the war. *But he lost me so it's me who's really winning.*

My musings were interrupted by Tee's self-confident voice. "I know who and what I work for and trust me, you are gonna get some feels. All I ask is that you keep my connection to this a secret. Chuck's ass wanted one of his little stooges in the club to hook up with this guy and I didn't feel right about it. It seemed way too creepy to me."

"Creepy how?" Who the fuck was this dude, Obama? If I got to this room and saw Barack's ass trying to creep on Mother Michelle, me and the Secret Service were gonna get into it.

"He's doing a trial just like you are. I thought two newbies together would work better than two who were experienced. Besides, he's not famous, but he's rich. Like richer than you rich. Which is saying a lot."

My eyes rolled because everyone had their perceptions of me, including my friends. They weren't exactly wrong, but still. I made my way into the garage and put all of my things in the backseat.

"You know better than anyone that I work hard. Why else would I have need for a service like this?" I hit the button to lift the garage as I cranked the car still mentally psyching myself up for this and attempting to regain some of my bravado after Tee's creepy comment threw me off track.

Her sarcastic laugh boomed through my Bluetooth as I backed out of the garage.

"You're not actually in need of the service. You're basically whoring us out to serve your own personal needs of instant validation from the opposite sex in a controlled environment that will keep you safe and hopefully leave you satisfied." Her words were spoken so matter of factly that I almost didn't take offense to them.

Almost.

Leave it to her brainiac ass to manage to put this situation into a perspective that was both accurate and insulting at the same damn time. That was my Tee, the multi-faceted shit stirrer.

"So you're my pimp now?"

She scoffed as the background noises started up again. "Technically, you're both the whore and the john if that makes sense."

My hand want to run my fingers through my hair in frustration but I was halted by the *hairmet.* Which only increased my annoyance. "You really must not want me to come at all."

"Nee, you have to." The plea was gone and she was now speaking in the types of absolutes that people in her profession often cautioned people against indulging.

"Why are you so desperate?" I stopped at a red light and was tempted to video chat her so I could read her facial expression. Her voice only gave away a hint of whatever was really going on and I needed the extra insight. I hated walking into any situation blind which was what made me so great at business.

She sighed and I felt like I was messing something up for her. What, I had no clue, but something big was obviously going on.

"Not desperate, but I agree this is what you need to do. You have major deals coming up in the next few months. The last thing you need is for Montez's ass to hold you back when he isn't even around. If it were up to me that house would be put on the market and you'd be heading back home. You only moved out there to help him follow his dreams. It's time that you do what you need to follow yours."

"Now is not the time for a pep talk, Tee." I was fronting not wanting to get in my emotions because I appreciated her words and her constant position in my corner. She wasn't a fan of Montez's either, but supported me in supporting him. I loved her even more for that.

She laughed and resumed her background noise symphony. "You knew I was going to add my two cents whether you wanted the coins or not. But my question right now is, are you still coming or not?"

I eased onto the interstate and was headed toward the airport. The Arlington traffic wasn't that bad and I would make it to the airport well before I needed to. I'd already set up a few things for the night so that I could have a semblance of control of what went on. Not knowing what to expect I needed something that I could rely on being a sure thing.

"Yeah, I'll be there. I've already had a hellacious last few months, what's the worst that could happen?"

"Just make sure he doesn't make your pussy speak."

My face frowned up because I was trying to figure out what in the hell she was saying. "Tee, what the actual fuck are you talking about?"

"I saw this meme the other day—"

"Why do so many of our conversations start off like this?"

She sucked her teeth before she continued. "Memes are the modern way for people to express themselves and their ideals. Stop being so damn antiquated."

"Forgive me for not wanting to take life advice from a meme. That's like living my life by a damn fortune cookie."

"Bitch, you better start playing them numbers!"

"Tee, focus! The meme?"

"Oh, yeah. The meme said that if you look a man in his eyes and his look makes your pussy speak you've found for your sexmate. I wish all of that for you tonight."

I shook my head in disbelief. If I was a meme I would be that Shannon Sharpe one right about now. "I knew I shouldn't have asked you to elaborate."

"Whatever, bitch. Catch your flight and I'll see you Saturday. Hopefully late as fuck and walking with a limp."

I couldn't help but giggle and be hopeful that her words were some type of sexual prophecy and she'd done me right by hooking me up with whoever this was I was meeting.

"Bye, Tee."

CHAPTER TWO

Hour One

Him

"Yo, you really doing this though?"

If this were any other situation where someone was questioning why I was making a decision, someone would be getting fired. The incredulous sound of his voice as he asked the question was rooted in him thinking I wasn't intelligent enough to make a sound decision. Which was unacceptable. But this time, I couldn't even be mad. I was about to do some crazy shit.

Extra crazy.

Some shit my mama would probably beat my ass for if she found out.

Ain't no probably, she would definitely beat my ass and not give a damn about it.

I leaned back in the custom built leather office chair and steepled my hands in front of me. I gave a look to the owner of the voice that should've conveyed *leave this situation the fuck alon*e but apparently, his normally sharp interpersonal skills were turned off at the moment. Or he was more worried about getting his point across than keeping his job. Of course his job was to help me protect my brand so maybe he was doing both.

He stood there waiting, with his ever present tablet in hand, on me to answer his question. Like *he* was the fucking boss and I was the employee. *Ain't this about a bitch.*

"Since when do you get the right to question what the hell it is I do?" One thing I didn't do was pull that boss shit, although I was always on my boss shit. And not in the way people acted once they got a few zeros in the bank and some clout they could lose when their fifteen minutes of fame were up.

My shit was legit, generational, multi-national—to the point where I stayed under the radar as much as possible so that people could keep out my damn business.

A shifting of his feet was the only sign that he thought he might have crossed the line. His concern was quickly dispelled because instead of backing off like a normal person would do when the person who cut their check was obviously displeased with their actions, he decided to press forward—and press his luck.

"I'm just trying to make it make sense is all." His peanut butter skin was flushed slightly and I knew it was from him trying to hold tight to what he really wanted to say. Not like I gave a fuck if he spoke his mind. If he was bold enough to speak up, he would be bold enough to accept whatever the consequences would be. It was just that simple.

I studied his face waiting on the telltale signs of his discomfort to rear their heads: hand running over his close-cropped curls, a tug on his beard, or his thumb flicking across his nose defiantly— none of those happened. So, I knew he was serious about continuing on with this conversation.

"Why does what I do personally have to make sense to you at all?" My hands stayed steepled and I took a deep breath before I spoke in order to maintain the even-tone I was known for. Internally I was reminding myself that if I swung I didn't want to pay the worker's comp claim that would come along with assaulting his ass.

Fool is lucky my ass doesn't feel like looking for yet another assistant.

He looked at me and I saw the concern which was ironic because he brought this to me in the first place. "I'm not attempting to tell you how to run your life, but the fallout of something like this being made public—"

My hands finally relaxed and I picked up my phone to continue clearing work so that I could enjoy my evening.

"This is a private matter and a private service. Help me understand who or what is going to be finding out shit about what I'm doing. Have you not done your due diligence on the company and the candidate? It was you who brought it to my attention in the first place. Should I start checking behind you now?"

He shot me a look that conveyed he was fully insulted by me questioning his thoroughness, but hell, so was I. I didn't get to where I was by being sloppy or making dumb decisions. Risky, yes, but never reckless. *This nigga had me fucked up.*

"Of course I did. I have transferred everything over to you with her information redacted as you requested."

I wasn't worried about speaking freely in my office. I had it swept weekly for bugs and only devices that were encoded with a specific and unique chip could work within these walls. I'd taken extreme caution in maintaining my privacy which was why I didn't get him questioning me. His eyes were either glued on me or the black tufted leather wall behind my head. I was just happy he wasn't looking down at his damn feet.

"Medical records?"

"The ones that were provided by the service were deemed accurate, but we had a little bird hack into a few systems just to double check and ensure that what we were given was accurate." He smiled triumphantly and although it was good to be pleased with yourself, he was starting to think he needed to advise me. *Well, that just wouldn't do.*

"Raph, do you like your job?"

He rolled his eyes and dropped his formal demeanor. He crossed his arms across his chest and tucked his tablet under one arm. He was more than welcome to sit his ass down in one of the leather club chairs in front of my desk, but he seemed to thrive on formality while we were in the office. Stupid, but whatever got shit done, made him happy, and kept my shit on point was fine with me.

My eyes strayed to the solid African Blackwood wall to my left. It was built to capture the light from the wall of windows that displayed a skyline view at my right. That one wall cost almost half a million dollars to fully panel but the effect was beautiful and worth every penny.

"Bruh, are we back on this? I'm a fucking MBA, man. I'm here to learn at your knee. Of course I love my job but forgive me for thinking that part of me being the person that keeps your secrets and orders your life means I can let you know when you're about to do something crazy."

"Have I ever made an investment and not checked the shit out thoroughly?"My head tilted cockily to the side of its own volition. My mama would've blamed it on the arrogance in my DNA and she wouldn't have exactly been wrong. Now that I was past the formalities with Raphael I could hurry this conversation up so I could begin the one thing I'd been looking forward to for a minute.

He finally relaxed enough to sit his ass down in a chair. He did it with a huff because he was clearly frustrated with me. My life was full of ironies. "No, but—"

My hand went up to stop him because that question should have obviously been rhetorical. "So why would anything be different now?"

The look on his face was incredulous as he stared at me silently for a moment. He took so long I was about to give his ass permission to speak but he finally found his voice. "Because you don't need to do this, man. You can legit pull like every bad bitch on the planet. Why in the hell are you using a service that matches you up with someone for the night?"

He was under the impression like everyone else that simply because I had money meant that I had no problems. I'd learned from a young age that having money only meant you didn't have to worry about your bills being paid. And that was only if your ass lived within your means. If you didn't, then you were susceptible to the same stressors as everyone else. Money didn't mean shit. Especially when you were interested in authenticity in each interaction. The people with the most money often fronted like those who had the least. It was a constant battle of trying to one-up one another. The shit was tiring.

Deciding to answer him instead of coming off as annoyed as I really was, I leaned back in my seat. My life was all about keeping up the veneer and right now was no different. Few people were privy to my feelings and as close as we were, Raph wasn't one of them. At least not about this area of my life.

"According to Chuck, this is an experience for wealthy men who want to be catered to but don't have the time, energy, or effort to put into dating. It's not some escort bullshit where the bitches could have an agenda because the people they set you up with have as much to lose as anyone else in the club. Spend your life dodging gold-diggers and you'd understand why this shit is vital to anyone in the ten to one percent."

I wasn't wrong. There were plenty of people I knew, hoteliers, business moguls, tech geniuses, athletes, and the like who didn't know how to decipher the wheat from the chaff. Some of them had gotten caught up with chicks they thought were cool but ended up being baby mamas from hell. My family was old school. You knocked a woman up? You gave her your last name. Wasn't no co-parenting shit with my folks. And to be honest I didn't want that either. Whenever my life settled down, *I* wanted to settle down. Find a woman I could spoil and have her pop out some babies that were the perfect mix of us. But being who I was, that wasn't the type of life anyone expected me to want. I was a playboy, an international one at that, so women were willing to do whatever they could to get at me. And some of them had done some extra crazy shit.

Which was why I spent a fucking fortune each year on security.

"While you're over here trying to talk me out of this shit, did you have everything sent over to the room like I requested?" He didn't have to say he didn't approve of the lengths I was going to it was evident by the look on his face. It was laughable that he thought his visual disapproval would somehow prevent me from doing what the fuck I wanted to anyway.

"Yes I did. Down to the La Perla made to fit her measurements and the handbags that you ordered. If this isn't some escort shit, why is the room stocked with condoms and you ordering lingerie?"

He had completely dropped the boss/employer façade and was once again just being a friend. Which was why I didn't mind answering his question this time.

"A nigga can hope right? Besides, escorts get paid to fuck, this is some rich people club type shit where everyone is on the same page. I requested the girlfriend experience, and if I had one, this would be the shit I'd do for her."

His eyes cut back toward me from where he had been admiring the view of the city. "Boss, you spent like six hours on your way back from Tokyo approving these gifts for a woman you don't know. You sure you'll be able to leave this at the door come tomorrow?"

"I won't have any other choice now will I?"

We were in a silent stare off and his look was far too thoughtful for my liking. I thought my comment would end whatever thought was in his head, but he still had that look on his face like he wanted to say something else.

"What?" There was no need to try and keep the annoyance out of my voice. He knew he was pissing me off, might as well let him dig his own grave.

"Is this one of those moments where I can speak freely and my job not be in jeopardy or am I sitting here on the verge of being fired?"

I waved him off letting him know I wasn't on some tyrant shit. "You're good for now."

"I guess that depends on what it is I have to say, huh?" His smirk let me know I should've ended the conversation here but being the glutton for punishment I was, I encouraged him to continue.

"Pretty much."

"I think that you're making a mistake." *Well that was obvious.* "But not for the reason you think."

Now he had my attention and I wanted to hear more. Probably the reason why he said the shit the way he did.

"Enlighten me."

He sighed as he sat back in the leather chair and placed his foot on his knee. He had the nerve to be wearing argyle socks with his Berluttis and a bowtie. It was like he wanted someone to liken him to Farnsworth Bentley. Like this was the uniform for his current role and he wanted people to recognize that shit.

"You are a decent man, boss. Decent in the way that you might get caught up with this person and you might enjoy this experience too much."

I chuckled and began to flip my cellphone in my hand absentmindedly. "Isn't that the point? To get lost in the fantasy?" This was hitting a little too close to the wall my emotions were kept behind, but I decided to hear him out.

His stare was intense and I knew I was going to be convicted with what came out of his mouth next. "But when do the lines blur?"

In an attempt to continue to appear unbothered I shrugged my shoulders and stilled my hand.

"Read off what you know about this woman. Not her name address or anything like that, read what makes her sound like a gold digger." His concern came from no where so I wanted to hear the justifications for his words.

I knew he'd memorized her information, at least what was pertinent, because he didn't batt an eye or connect with his iPad. "To be honest, nothing does."

"So what's the problem? Is her information false?"

"No..." His eyes diverted from mine and back to the leather wall just over my head.

Curiosity compelled me to question him further. "What is it then?"

His gaze returned to mine unwavering with a strength and surety of self that reminded me why I'd hired him in the first place. "I think you might like her."

I huffed sarcastically, annoyed that I'd been this involved in a conversation that had no merit. "Isn't that the point?'

His iPad was now in his lap and he waved a hand in front of him with a smirk of knowing on his face.

"No, like really like her. A lot. You guys are completely compatible. You might fuck around and fall in love when this is supposed to be a one-time thing."

"No one can fall in love in one night."

His eyebrow raised and that same look of arrogant confidence in his words graced his face. "As many times as you've done the impossible, are you really sure you believe that?"

His words sent something, not necessarily a chill but an intense awareness, down my spine. As though his words were prophetic and I needed to heed him. Or back out of this in its entirety in order to save myself somehow. I wanted to chop him in his damn throat to wipe the smirk off his face but I kept my hands to myself.

"This will be the one time I don't defy the odds."

**

This is a whole ass lie. Must be a setup.

I'd rented the penthouse suite of the Warren Hotel in Buckhead. The views were amazing and there was a balcony that wrapped around the entire suite. True to the brand, the interior was immaculate. It was done in what I could only describe as a vintage chic type of feel. The walls were slate gray throughout with black and white paintings on the walls. The flooring was hickory, stained a dark ebony. The suite consisted of a foyer, a great room, formal dining room, a full kitchen with keeping room and eat-in area, three bedrooms and four bathrooms. I was standing in the great room marveling at the woman that security had just allowed into my temporary sanctuary.

There was no way that this woman needed to be here with me right now. Something had to be wrong with her. Of course I'd done my due diligence and had Chuck send me a picture of the woman he'd matched me with via his...service. I was glad for the last minute change his lead agent sent over because the first chick didn't do it for me. I'd taken it a step further and had more in-depth information gathered on her so that I could give myself peace of mind. But the photos that had been gathered from her social media and other sites did her absolutely no justice.

She had the type of shape that women envied and men lusted over. Not the kind that bore the markings of a surgeon's hand with proportions that were so unrealistic they made the body look abnormal, but the kind that the Almighty handcrafted with careful and purposeful craftsmanship so that the man who won her appreciated his prize for a life well lived.

What in the hell was wrong with me?

The direction my mind traveled made me feel as though Raph's words were coming back to bite me in the ass. Or he'd jinxed me and now my mind wouldn't move off the shit he'd said. The immediate desire to praise her came with an ease that made my thoughts of her seem reflexive. And my desire—no, my *need* to be the man gifted with her increased exponentially.

Baby girl was beautiful though. And not in that carefully contrived, just for now kind of way. She was beautiful in an earthy way. Authentic. Hips that flared out from a small waist, not tiny by today's standard but with a significant enough dip to give her body that hourglass feel, and an ass that I could see from the front and the thick ass thighs to match. Her amber-colored skin was flawless and looked like she'd bathed in nothing but shea butter, coconut oil, and the tears of angels her entire life. It was smooth, and blemish free…and inviting. Her hair was different and I knew immediately that it wasn't hers. I had not a fuck to give about what most women did with their hair, but this gray shit that flowed down her back rang false. Like this wasn't who she was on a day-to-day basis and had attached this shit to her person in order to conceal her identity or to be someone she wasn't.

Or to please me, thinking that whatever she had naturally wouldn't suffice.

The two almond-shaped orbs she called her eyes sparkled like they held the light of a star within them and were embedded into a face that held both full cheeks and dimples. A small mole graced the top of her heart shaped full lips; her fuller lower lip looked primed for me to suck on. She reminded me of Michelle Thomas, the actress that played Myra Munkhouse on Family Matters. She looked wholesome. And so goddamn beautiful.

She walked in confidently, but I could almost smell the nerves radiating off her. Her legs were bare and seemed to go on for miles. I wasn't the tallest in the world at just over six-feet, but even in her heels I had a few inches on her.

And those gotdamn heels were about to make me speed up this

getting to know you timeline.

I had a thing for sexy footwear. I blamed it on my childhood spent being forced to go on photoshoots and shit. There was no part of a woman that I didn't admire and I was a sucker for a pretty face. But a beautiful set of legs, and pretty feet encompassed in sexy shoes did something to me.

Like having me sitting here wanting to strip this outfit off a woman I didn't even know so that I could fuck her from behind with those heels on.

"What's your name, love?"

I figured I would break the ice since she'd spent as much time staring at me as I had at her. Which pleased the part of me that was happy to be admired for my physical appearance and not my bank account. Call it shallow, but there were times when you wanted to feel attractive to the opposite sex. Being who I was, I never knew if people's intentions were altruistic or not. Normally not.

She shifted and seemed to squeeze those thick thighs of her together in the outfit she had on that was a blend of professional and *come fuck me* before she responded.

"Tonight, it's whatever you'd like it to be." Even her voice was sensual. Low with a slight rasp that turned my thoughts devious. I could almost hear her moaning in my ear as I pounded into her.

She talked a good game and had the coyness down to a science but it wasn't her. I had to trust my instincts above all else and with every fiber of my being I knew this chick in front of me was a good girl. Part of me felt bad that she was at this place, being used by this service to provide comfort to someone. Because of how the service ran, I knew that the majority of the people in it had amassed some type of wealth. There was a minimum threshold of pedigree one had to have in order to even know this existed. I just couldn't believe someone like her needed to be here. Maybe her family had the breeding but not the funding. Whatever her story, I was sad she was going through something but happy because she was here and available for me.

I perused her appearance again and noticed that times couldn't have been too tough. She wore an expensive and intricately woven necklace that was either platinum or white gold. Or both. The luster of the metal reflected its purity and I was intrigued by the design. It was primitive, polished, and tickled some memory of the past I couldn't quite access.

The interwoven diamonds and triangles were something that I'd seen before but I couldn't remember where. She bit her lip causing the two dimples in her cheeks to pop out and my concern for her necklace and the matching bracelet vanished as my desire for her renewed. Well it never dissipated; it was simply pushed to the back while curiosity was thrust to the forefront. But now, it reminded me of why I was here.

Chuck hit it out of the park with this idea.

My anonymity was crucial in this exchange so I could only smirk at the answer she gave me.

Allowing my eyes to roam over her figure again I allowed my eyes to meet hers.

"Tonight you're my Heaven."

She chuckled slightly and it made me want in on the joke.

"Not original enough?" Maybe I was so used to people giving me bullshit I hadn't realized that I wasn't as humorous as they all made me think I was. Maybe I'd fallen into the trap that all men with money eventually did; thinking that we were God's gift to everything so we never really had to work for much. Especially when it came to the opposite sex. *Am I really that jaded? Shit, I'll have to tell mom she was right.*

Seeing as how Heaven appeared to be an impartial party, I pressed her for the honesty that no one else would give me. "What did I say that was so bad?"

Her shoulders shrugged in the way that let me know it was a reflex and she didn't care that some people thought the gesture unladylike. There were no airs about her, no pretenses and I knew she would give me the truth.

"Just makes me curious." Her eyes took in her surroundings and I could tell by her expression that she liked the decor.

That only led me to ask another question. "About?"

She turned so I could get the benefit of the glory of her face head on. I marveled again at how ordinarily beautiful she was. In the sweet kind of way that you normally didn't associate with sex appeal but she somehow managed it without issue. Her hips leaned against the loveseat and she eyed me not with suspicion, but with something akin to reserve.

"About how anonymous all of this really is." The darting of her tongue out to dampen her lip distracted me from her statement. But only for a moment.

My eyebrows dipped slightly and I was confused at her words. Did she know something about this that I didn't? I wanted to question her further, but decided to keep the comment to myself. She proceeded to walk toward the door and my heart squeezed for a moment thinking that she was walking out. But when she bent to pick up the large cooler bag and the handle of her rolling suitcase, I relaxed.

Being the man my father raised me to be, I stood from my place on the sofa, took the suitcase from her and, presumptively, rolled into the bedroom where my things already were. My security let me know she'd arrived alone and had traveled here from the airport, so she wasn't local and there was no off chance that I'd run into her again.

She hadn't moved from the spot where I'd taken her luggage from her. I wasn't sure if it was because she was stunned or she was waiting on my chivalry to continue, but either way I picked up the heavy cooler bag and walked toward the massive kitchen. Sitting the whole thing on the counter not bothering to ask questions, I turned back toward her.

"What are your expectations for the night?" She'd kept the heels on but had made herself more comfortable by opening a bottle of cognac from the bar. I was at least happy that she'd relaxed a little. Or that she was drinking something that would help her do so.

"Tonight is all about desire."

She walked further into the room and my eyes stayed glued to her shape. The sound of her voice was hypnotic and had a soft inflection of something, maybe French, in its tone. Like she had a parent that grew up in a foreign country, not France, but one where the French had colonized and they'd been forced to learn it. That memory was scratching at the nape of my neck again and yet, I couldn't access what it meant or why it was important.

Momentarily, I was at a loss for words. If anyone who knew me saw me in this position their mouths would be hanging open in shock. For me to stand stupefied by a woman would have made them question their previous claims of my impenetrability and inability to be fazed by anything.

I cleared my throat as I watched her examine her surroundings. Her lips meeting the edge of her glass emphasized the fullness of her mouth as it pressed against the crystal. The column of her throat looked more erotic as her head titled slightly to allow the liquor to flow. Unlike most women who attempted to hide their inner vixen, this woman was almost daring the part of her that was still innocent and untainted to remain hidden in order to give herself what she thought she needed.

"And what does that mean to you?" The glass went down on the black granite bar top and we resumed our stare off

"To be appreciated. Physically, emotionally—"

"What kind of men have you been around that haven't at least appreciated you physically?" If she wanted to be desired I for damn sure had no problem with flattery. Hell, I spoke it fluently and wielded it often in order to succeed. Why should this be any different than my other transactions? This was business after all, with pleasure thrown in the mix.

I thought I heard her mutter *you'd be surprised* but she cleared her throat without meeting my eyes.

"As I was saying I just want to be desired. In all ways."

"I can understand that." And I could. Hell, I was here for the same reason. I didn't need the physical part of the appreciation, but I wanted someone's opinions of me to not be tainted by a stock report or an uptick in my financials.

Brazenly, she leaned forward giving me a view of the more than ample cleavage that strained at the neckline of her v-neck shirt.

"So tell me, why is it that you want from this weekend?"

"A girlfriend."

The shock of my words must have been too much because her mouth opened and closed about four times before she narrowed her eyes at me curiously.

"You were serious about that?"

I crossed my arms over my chest as I let a playful smile cross my face. "Completely. I can always pay someone to care, to play a role, but I figured if I were looking to engage in something that was mutually satisfactory with no strings attached, truly? I'd want someone who could care for me without looking for the benefit they could gain by doing so."

Her eyebrows raised damn near to her hair line and a flush of color imbued her already radiant skin. I found out the reason why when she spoke again.

"And what about sex?"

Not knowing her angle or the reason she was here I studied her for a moment. She seemed sincere in her request yet nervous for posing it. She had all the hallmarks of being uncomfortable, the shifting of her feet, the flush of color, and the nervous energy as she awaited my answer. But she was looking me dead in my face so I knew her ass was serious.

Maybe that was what she needed more than anything. That feeling of being desired absolutely. I was now sure she'd said what I thought she had earlier and someone had fucked up her self-esteem. She was probably in the same position as me not knowing why people really wanted her.

Intriguing.

I cleared my throat and prepared to answer her the best way I knew how.

CHAPTER THREE

Hour Three

Heaven

"So what about sex?"

I attempted to keep my voice even and its cadence normal as I asked the question, but I was annoyed by the way he was beating around the bush. Annoyed because it was making me feel a level of respect that I hadn't imagined would come with an experience like this. I thought for sure that this would be a talk about what we liked and disliked in the bedroom and then a few hours of having my back blown out.

I got the bullshit that Tee was selling about the service, but I thought it was just that—bullshit. A way for older, horny, homely people to get their rocks off. Or for people who had kinks that were too extreme to discuss with someone in their life. But this dude was talking... romance.

Realism.

I didn't know if I could do realism when I had come to play a role. To wear the confidence I used to possess so effortlessly like a second skin and hope, that after all of this, it would give my ego the jumpstart that it so desperately needed. My creativity was being stifled and I needed that edge...that swagger back that I'd had when I felt like I had everything in the world at my fingertips. And once I got it on my own, there was no way in the world I would allow myself to predicate my worth on my ability to hold what society deemed a *good man*. I needed to find the light I'd lost when I got lost in being an *us* and forgot all about keeping any part of myself intact.

"If you were my girlfriend, I'd like to think you found me physically attractive enough to want to fuck me."

Why did he have to curse? He'd been doing such a good job of keeping up this façade of the polite, elitist Adonis, and now...Mr. Perfect seemed to have some rough edges I wanted to snuggle up to.

Down bitch. Every woman had an inner ho. At least Tee always said that but I never believed her. Until now. I didn't think I was granted one when I became of age. At least not before. I wasn't necessarily frigid in bed, just...unenthused. At least according to my ex. He wouldn't hear of doing the types of things I liked but thought staid, boring sex was enough to get me off. Missionary was fine for lovemaking but sometimes a bitch liked her ass spanked. *Oh the verbal abuse I endured over that level of transparency.*

But hearing him say the word fuck from the two bow-shaped portals to what I was sure was a very capable—and strong—tongue must have deactivated whatever hibernating my inner ho had been doing because she was doing cartwheels in my walls and A-Town stomping my clit, causing it to pulsate and shoot tingles throughout my entire body. I'm talking nipples hardening; goosebumps covering my body, and even my damn scalp tingled. That of course could be the hairmet but I was blaming it on him.

Who was I kidding, this man was fine. Like extra, extra fine. *If this night goes well I'm up to taking his ass to Red Lobster, fine.*

Names had yet to be exchanged but the only word that I could come up to describe him was to call him Adonis. He was visually stunning to look at. Butterscotch colored skin that had a glow about it making it look like he regularly exfoliated and had someone on hand to keep his nut sack empty. Men only got that look by being sexually satisfied and well taken care of. So why was he here? That was a question I doubted I would find the answer to. His skin was butterscotch, mixed with multiple hues of gold that almost made him sparkle. *Who knew niggas had sparkly skin?*

His hair was cut low but with waves so deep I knew he was on the verge of needing a haircut despite the precision of his edge up. He was about a millimeter away from his coal black locks going from a deep wave to a full on curl.

He had on clothing that spoke to his norm being far more stuffy than what he had on. I could tell that he thought his jeans, button up, blazer and loafers were casual wear but part of me was dying to see this man draped in nothing but gray sweatpants and a white tank. Maybe some Nike slides and socks to complete the look. But this dressed down look was more business casual instead of regular casual.

Reminding me that we weren't friends and that this arrangement was anything but the norm. At least for me.

Maybe he really was this uptight or maybe he thought he needed to impress me. Either way I needed him to relax. Of course I hadn't exactly dressed down myself so I couldn't blame him. Against his golden skin his eyes looked almost black and slightly feminine because of the heavy fringe of lashes that encircled them. Add thick black eyebrows that sat as two sentinels over his expressive eyes and they were the focal point of his face.

In a nutshell, he was the essence of Black male excellence and I had to fold my lips together when I looked at him to ensure that my ass wasn't drooling. Because I for damn sure wanted to.

I cleared my throat unsure of how to proceed from here. It wasn't awkward this tension that flowed around, it was the kind that would build until it found its release. My suspicion was that a release would only be found in the bedroom.

"Let me get started on dinner."

His brows furrowed and one hand went to his chin to stroke his goatee.

"You cook?"

"It might be foreign to you, but some people actually prepare their own meals." I winced at how prejudiced I sounded. "Sorry, that wasn't a dig, I was simply—"

He laughed me off as though he agreed with my sentiment. "If I were any other person that you'd met through this setup you'd probably be spot on. I unfortunately am one of the normal ones. Or abnormal if you think about it." His look was pensive as he reflected on his words.

"I thought you wanted a girlfriend?" When I saw what his goal for the night was, I took it to mean some kinky shit. Like let him tie me up without complaint or have a safe word in case he got too weird. Like fifty shades of bondage.

And yet you still brought your Black ass here didn't you?

He nodded his agreement before he spoke yet I knew he was about to challenge what I'd just said. "Yes, girlfriend. Not maid. Not private chef. If my girl was cooking for me, I damn sure would be next to her in some capacity. My love language is touch so I am very hands on. In the kitchen, and out." The glimmer in his eye let me know he was being flirtatious just incase I'd missed the innuendo in his words. His eyebrow ticked upward momentarily as if he was attempting to keep his face neutral and failing. The momentary flash of bravado did nothing but increase the pulsing of need between my thighs. From the moment I'd walked in he had put jumper cables on my libido and sent shock waves through my clit. Electrical pulses that rocked through me each time his eyes met mine.

It was my turn to nod and then all but scurry my ass into the kitchen. My heels were going to be a pain in my ass so I took them off and washed my hands. He'd followed behind me and joined me at the center island.

"What are we making tonight?"

His question jarred me from my musings and I couldn't help but stare at him as I gathered my thoughts. "I figured something hearty would do for tonight so I was going to make stew."

That eyebrow shot up without thought yet again and he studied me from head to toe. I was sure that my outfit didn't give him the comfort in knowing that I could move around the kitchen. But me being well put together did not mean I couldn't burn.

Ignoring the look on his face, I decided to check out the kitchen to make sure I had everything I needed. Whoever designed it needed a raise because it was one of the most beautiful spaces I'd ever seen. The dark ebony flooring extended into this space offsetting the veining in the Calcutta gold marble waterfall island. The island cabinetry was black and the perimeter cabinets were a stark white with the same marble on the center island and backsplash. The appliances were hidden but the pendant lights and cabinet hardware were brushed gold to coordinate with the marble. It was beautiful in its simplicity.

Unpacking the items I'd had delivered and waiting for me at the front desk, I began to arrange our dinner. This hotel literally had everything and when I asked for an Instant Pot, they were more than happy to oblige and provide one for me.

"Is this something you've done often?" My eyes looked up from the steak I was cubing and I couldn't help but smile at him. I mean, he'd carefully worded that question so that I would have to try hard to be offended. For someone I didn't know to be careful with my emotions, no matter the reason, was the first brick in place of edifying my foundation. *And to think you just said your self-worth wouldn't be based on a man.*

Technically it wasn't based on him, but it was a nice little ego stroke.

Since he looked the type to only date women who could order well, I decided not to take offense.

"I've been cooking food since I was a little girl. You don't sneed to worry. Unless you don't eat beef, then you're going to have to order room service." With a smile I nodded toward the television that was mounted on the wall inside the kitchen. "You mind cutting that on and putting it on MSNBC? I know I'm not supposed to be doing any work, but there is an announcement I've been waiting on hearing."

Those eyebrows shot up in surprise yet again as he silently obliged. I was happy that he was honoring the rules and not asking me for more information. If I wanted to divulge it I would, but I also knew that Tee's job was on the line if things got out of hand. I wouldn't risk her professional standing simply because I felt the need to run off at the mouth.

My eyes were glued to the screen as I watched the stock ticker going at the bottom of the screen. I needed to look into commodities because that would determine what price my next shipment would be brought in at. The taxes that this new government of ours had decided to impose were utter bullshit. We were supposed to be a government about business but they did everything to stifle entrepreneurship at every turn.

"Mind if I open a bottle?" He drew my eyes to him and I watched as he held up two bottles of wine.

"By all means."

"Preference?" My eyes went back to his face and he was actually waiting on me to answer. I thought his question was a formality or a way to challenge my opinion but he truly wanted an answer.

"Red if you have it. It'll go better with dinner."

"My kind of lady. Most women want white because it's light and crisp."

"What red do you have?" He walked toward the wine fridge that was built into the corner of the kitchen. Pulling out a bottle from the shelf stocked with many he held it up triumphantly.

"Shiraz." Now he was my kind of guy. Most men would select a pinot noir because they assumed women wanted the lighter more aromatic pinot. I liked the full-bodied dry flavor of the shiraz. It went with my personality.

"Pour it up."

"Are you able to reveal why you're interested in this?" He kept his eyes on his task as though he was preventing me from being intimated by his question. As if he couldn't be more perfect, the man even had great taste in crystal. The Riedel Sommeliers 260th Anniversary Burgundy glasses were a pair I'd been eyeing for myself. *Tee is really good at her damn job.*

"Should I not be?" His eyes met mine and a curious look now graced his face. Seeing that my hands were still he sat the glass down next to me.

"Most beautiful women aren't into stocks and tariffs."

I couldn't help but chuckle and feel sorry for him. "You've been hanging out with the wrong set of beautiful women then." The meat I'd been cubing up now went into the pot and I washed my hands before I picked up the glass.

"Apparently so. A toast to a beautiful night ahead of us." He tapped my glass with his and gave me a smile that could only be described as panty-wetting. *He's a veritable god this one.*

I sipped and weighed how I could be forthright without divulging too much information about myself. "I know we can't do the whole *tell me about yourself* type of thing, but my business is affected by the issues in the newly formed United Countries of Africa. I needed to check on a few commodities and what they're trading at and see if this fool we have as a president will make the right decision when it comes to setting up full-fledged trade agreements with them."

He nodded his head in understanding and kept his fingers on his wine glass. His eyes roamed my frame and then stopped at my hands watching as threw spices into the pot.

"You might actually know what you're doing."

"Not that I'm one to give credence to stereotypes, but I am one Black woman you should trust in the kitchen."

We exchanged small smiles and our eyes gravitated toward the TV. "This might be what you were waiting for."

"The latest on the move the United States has made to block effective trade with the newly formed UCA has taken an unexpected turn. Where it was once believed that the president would be able to block the expansion of the agreement and impose higher tariffs on those looking to do business directly with the company, the move has been vetoed by Congress. This means that trade has been expanded to the area and only time will tell what additional fees, fines or taxes will be levied in the future. Back to you guys in the studio."

* * *

The news was good for me and for business. It meant that y next phase of development was going to move forward without a hitch. Adonis was staring thoughtfully at the screen as if he too had a dog in this fight. If he was at the status that I could assume he was by his mannerisms and style of dress, this type of trade would be lucrative for anyone who had the money to invest.

"I can almost see the chess pieces moving around in your head. Good news for you?" He smiled as my words took him out of his own thoughts.

"Good news for everyone. It has been historically unfair the way that the entire continent of Africa has been looked down upon as the scourge of the world when colonialists and opportunists routinely rape her of her natural resources, fund wars that will keep the continent in an uproar, and back oppressive regimes. The countries uniting as one will do more for the expansion of wealth within their borders and halt the perception that has existed for so long. Africa as a whole is a land filled with riches, it about time that the people who live there reaped some of the benefit."

The tears that had unknowingly filled my eyes began to blur my vision. It was so beautiful to hear someone that had no connection, at least that I knew of, root so hard for a place and its success. So many of us were disconnected from what was happening on the continent that we all came from that we allowed our brethren to suffer. To hear this man that should only be concerned with the financial opportunities speak to the need for the *people* who'd survived the atrocities visited upon their nations to come out on top moved me in a way that I hated for him to witness.

"Did I upset you?" He'd moved closer to me and the perplexed look on his face made me realize that he couldn't decipher my reaction to his words.

I cleared my throat and shook my head wiping the one tear that fell from my cheek.

"No, upset isn't the way I would describe how I feel in this moment. I'm touched in a way that words can't begin to explain. Being born here but having a father that is an immigrant has always altered the perception that I had of anything that happened in the Motherland. But to hear someone speak about it as passionately as he does, inspires me. For you to be so young and to care not about your bottom line but that other people are succeeding, it is a beautiful thing to hear."

His cheeks suffused with heat as the golden color of his skin darkened to an almost amber and it took me a moment to realize that he was blushing. Actually embarrassed by the praise I'd given him. For a man to be so successful it was shocking that he was so moved by my words.

"Thank you."

"I'm sorry...are you...are you blushing?" This moment called for some kind of levity because I felt like I'd revealed a little piece of my soul in getting so emotionally caught up in his words. So if I had to tease him to pivot out of depths this conversation was falling into, I definitely would.

His face grew redder as he swiped a hand down it. He wasn't able to hid his smile even as he licked his lips attempting to play it off. "You just gonna call me out on the shit?"

His embarrassment somehow made him all the more endearing to me. "I'm saying, you a light bright so it would be difficult to hide the shit."

"You not gonna let me live a li'l bit? Just pretend I'm not over here all flushed up and shit?"

"Naw, player. Girlfriends tease, right? I think I'm going for full-fledged authenticity in our interactions this evening."

"Are you now?" That eyebrow quirk and smirk combo made another appearance and my mind skimmed back over what I said to see what had him so intrigued. It was my turn to be embarrassed but luckily for me my melanin kept that shit hidden. His eyes glanced at the food I'd been assembling this whole time and he looked from my hands back to my eyes. "You done with all this?"

I nodded as I went to the sink to wash my hands. "Yeah, still worried that it's going to kill you?"

"I've had attempts on my life before. This would by far be the more pleasurable way to go. Besides, this shit smells good as fuck and it ain't even done yet. I'm sure you're good."

"*Barka*." I hadn't realized I'd slipped into my father's tongue but he paid my *thanks*, that I'd spoken in Mossi, no mind and simply smiled back without questioning me. I eyed him strangely wondering what kind of nigga that Tee had paired me up with. Instead of giving me the benefit of additional information that I was obviously wanting, he moved from his place at the bar and walked around the island to where I stood. Reaching around he slowly removed the apron I'd tied around myself and let it fall to the floor. His hands lingered at my sides and I could feel the heat that bounced from his hands penetrating my clothing. His head hovered close to my neck and each exhale he released tickled my skin with his warm, humid breath.

"So I don't have to get the little paper and ask *do you want to be my girl check yes or no*. You ready to be all in already, huh?"

"I'm yours for tonight." When I spoke he leaned back and looked into my eyes. I noticed that they weren't as black as they originally appeared but a deep coffee with no cream with darker flecks in them. They seemed to study my eyes for something. Sincerity, some deeper meaning, or searching to see if I was hiding some ulterior motive. His hands stopped hovering on my sides as he reached down and took my hands in his.

"You trust me?" Those eyes were still watching me intently.

I couldn't help but smile as his constantly questions seemed to be a way to affirm my allegiance in this roleplaying.

"Implicitly."

I assumed his smile matched mine as his eyes crinkled slightly at the corners and the shone more brightly than before. He laced his fingers with mine and began to pull me toward the living room. Although I was curious, this was fantasy and the more we played the part, the more the role began to feel familiar. Comfortable. Natural. Not simply because I had been in this position for someone else for over a year. My relationship with Montez had never been this easy. I always heeded the adage of anything worth having was worth working hard for, but I'd learned the hard way that shit shouldn't be a battle at every turn.

No, mys comfort was because of this man. Or least his ability to convince me I was safe with him, this situation, and the roles we were going to play for one another. It wasn't going to be me giving and not receiving. He seemed as eager to pour into me on a soul level as my weary spirit was eager to receive. The desire I had to mean something to someone had taken control of my common sense but I didn't care. Adonis made me feel and after months of trying to numb my emotions because the negative ones overwhelmed everything, I was more than happy to let him cut a slice into the edifice that surrounded my emotions and let a few seep out. The nurturer in me wanted to provide him with what he needed. And the first thing was obviously trust. Despite my type A personality I left my control behind when I placed my hand in his.

We'd made it to the center of the room as he kept that small, almost unsure, smile on his face.

"Hey Jacq?" He called out the name with his eyes still focused on mine.

"Yes, sir?" I jumped hearing the voice respond that seemed to come from several different parts of the suite at once. He gripped me closer as if to attempt to assuage my fears. I wasn't worried, just startled. Well, maybe I was a little worried he had some random that was listening to everything we'd been discussing. *Should've asked Tee if they swept the room for bugs and cameras.*

He smiled at my surprise and my lack of questioning. "Play 'If Only for One Night' by Luther."

"Coming right up, sir." A noise chimed and then the opening melody of the song began to play through the speakers.

With an eyebrow raised quizzically I couldn't help but ask one question. "Jacq?"

"Virtual manservant."

I nodded because I was surprised and impressed all at once. "Is this some new age shit?"

"Not even on the market yet, love." The opening words of the song began and I felt caught up in the lyrics. Especially when Luther was crooning about being totally discreet. He held out a hand and although it was simple as hell it felt like the most debonair thing I'd ever experienced. "Dance with me?"

On their own volition, my feet began to move in sync with his. There was no hesitation or pretense as I allowed myself to be encompassed with all this *fine ass man* scent that seemed to erupt from his pores naturally. This was no smell that man had created nor could they duplicate. This scent was uniquely him. Clean, expensive and the type of realness that no one else could match. He was like a solid platinum gun; decadent and deadly. I knew I was playing Russian roulette getting involved in whatever this was, but as we swayed and he fit my body so firmly and familiarly to his, I could already feel my finger on the trigger.

May the odds be ever in my favor. But what is it I'm actually trying to avoid? Or run toward?

"Something on your mind?"

"This song takes me back." I smiled softly thinking of how this scene brought up feelings of déjà vu from my childhood.

"To? I know Black don't crack, but I doubt you were ever old enough to be courted when this song was popular." I wanted to roll my eyes at him but the endearing smile he wore on his face forced me to do nothing but push away from him slightly in mock offense. The band he called an arm was tight around me that I didn't put much, if any, distance between us. And what little space I'd created was once again enveloped as he fused us together. There was no *room for Jesus and the Holy Spirit* like nuns at Catholic schools try to enforce during coed dances.

"You trying to guess my age, Adonis?" Our lips hovered dangerously close to one another yet he didn't make a move. I refused to relinquish my position and he seemed incapable of forcing the issue. Which I would normally appreciate but being here in this room under this guise made the tension palpable between the two of us. Lust shimmered down on us like a continuous drizzle building humidity into the space we occupied and cloaking everything in its presence.

His eyebrow quirked at the moniker I'd placed on him and he didn't bother to request an explanation from me. I liked that he was confident enough within himself that he didn't need the external validation. It was something I was sure I could absorb through touch from him like I was Rogue from the X-Men. Take a little piece of his power and keep it with me long after this night ended. As long as that touch came vaginally.

More than one way to drain a man.

"Not about to get my ass reamed trying to guess. Either way up or down is an insult. I'm hoping you're not against telling me. I'll forget all the notions of *ladies first* in this instance and tell you mine instead. I'm almost thirty-seven."

My head reared back in surprise because nothing about this man said he was anywhere near forty. No touch of gray at the temples, none in the close cropped goatee on his face and not a wrinkle on his golden face.

"I'm sorry, say what?"

He leaned back and laughed, the sound infectious enough to force its way through my confusion and cause me to respond in kind. I mean, thirty-seven wasn't old, but here I was thinking he was younger than me. Plenty of people with bread still in their twenties nowadays. With a chuckle he pulled me ever closer to him and leaned over to my ear.

"In case you're wondering, I ain't had a problem with my dick since I first got some ass. You spread those legs and give me a chance to be inside of you, I'll show you what this grown ass man dick does."

My breathing hitched and then increased and with our proximity I knew he could feel my breath against the side of his face. As if his words didn't turn me on enough, he allowed his hand to graze the side of my face, the column of my neck and then pressed his lips against my collar bone.

That bitch Lauryn Hill LIED! There wasn't nothing sweet about this kiss. The way his full lips encompassed the object of his affection and his teeth grazed the skin of my clavicle, none of that could be classified as sweet.

Hot.

Wanting.

Sexy as fuck?

Yes, to all of the above.

But sweet? Hellllllll no. My thighs flexed together to try and keep the residual effect of his actions from becoming evident to him. Luther continued to croon in the background as my Adonis' hands dipped lower to mold the mounds of my breasts and my hands attempted to gain purchase on his shoulders. Knee buckling was always something that I thought happened to other women, but this man had me feeling weak in the knees.

Cue up the SWV playlist, Jacq.

He'd called me *Heaven* and in this moment I felt like he meant it. He touched me with reverence as if the privilege of entering me was something he'd worked for his entire life. Longed for. Sacrificed for. And at the end of a job well done was me and he was more than blessed by what he saw.

His exploration continued, but he stayed on top of my clothing as though he were awaiting a sign or simply enjoying the sweet torture his languid pace was giving me. I was never one to rush, but we'd been here for hours and I wanted to get to the part where I got my sexy back. His contact speeding up to slow down was creating a lot of tension, but it was also making me wonder what the hold up was.

As if he could read the direction of my thoughts, his hand caressed my lower body pulling it even more flush with his. And then **he** decided to join in on the party. There was no question of what was in his pants and whether or not it was happy to see me. That was a grown man dick he was toting and it was attempting to unleash itself through his zipper. If the outline was anything like the actual I would be limping out of here tomorrow.

All of this felt intimate. Far more involved than a simple turn in the sheets that I expected. The music, the caressing, the cooking, and the conversation. It was personal. The staring into my eyes he was doing made me realize he was serious about the desire for the girlfriend experience. To feel loved. And maybe for me, it was the same thing. To just be and be appreciated for the night.

Sex for me was always something extremely personal, but I was confident for this I could shut off my emotions. Especially since I'd expected for the person I was paired with to be subpar. Even with my bestie at the helm doing the choosing. But for the caresses that he delivered to penetrate not only my clothing but the barriers to all of my emotions. The looks into my eyes went deeper and began to unveil all of what I wanted to stay hidden. From him, the world, and hell, even myself. The vulnerability that was still there even after all this time. Weeks, months had passed and I was still struggling. Still bogged down in the bullshit of the past. With one look, one stroke of his hand against my cheek, he seemed to want to wipe all of that away. And his desire to be what I wanted and what I needed tonight made me all the more willing to submit to what he needed.

CHAPTER FOUR

Hour Five

Adonis

Her eyes widened as I kissed her before they fluttered close. As if she couldn't believe that, even after all this conversing we'd engaged in, I still found her attractive. In truth I desired her more now than I had when she'd walked in the door.

She didn't divulge what she did in-depth, but hearing the way she spoke about tariffs, exchange rates and the need for a healthier relationship with the United Countries of the Continent of Africa, she was smart. Not just *I received an MBA because all of the billionaire wives are doing it* smart, but the kind that came with being hands on in the day to day operations of running a company and also not being too good to be in the trenches alongside her people if they needed it.

It was a major turn on and furthered the play of the two sides to the woman before me.

I hadn't even slept with her yet and my mind was attempting to figure out how I could get a larger chunk of this agency than I'd initially thought to invest in. This woman spoke to me. Not the me that everyone saw, not even the philanthropic side of me, she spoke to the me that was buried beneath the veneer that even I had trouble separating from the image.

We'd eaten the dinner she'd prepared after dry-fucking one another in the middle of the massive living room. With each song that Jacq played, the mood bent more towards seduction than the getting to know her that I'd intended. The dinging of the contraption she'd prepared our food in was the only reminder that we had been moving toward something other than this being a typical one night stand. I could tell she had become slightly out of sorts with the direction things were flowing in. Either because she was too comfortable too soon, or she was a novice at all of this. I'd mastered the art of the fuck and duck a long time ago so I knew a rookie when I saw one. Heaven was a woman that reeked of loyalty, her very essence was derived from it, so I was guessing it was the latter that was throwing her.

Dinner had been more conversation about business, but not in a way where she was attempting to impress me with her knowledge, it was a discussion of a few observations that led into more. It didn't hurt that we'd both gotten a text alert concerning a massive increase in a mutual stock we'd invested in so we popped a bottle of champagne to celebrate our good fortune. That was what led us to the couch where I knew for a fact I didn't have much longer before I needed to be inside of her.

My hand went to caress her cheek but slid down the column of her neck to bring her even closer to me. A soft moan of what I hoped was ecstasy escaped her lips and I slipped my tongue in as they parted. Having one part of my anatomy tunneling into her moist depths made another long for the experience of her haven. I felt her hands grip the collar of the button down I wore as if my kiss alone rocked her to her core.

Good.

I didn't want to be the only one that was completely thrown off by feeling in this moment. This wasn't a regular feeling; it was something that was starting to make me question my levels of sanity. I was impressed by this woman. When I'd named her *Heaven,* it was purely for her physical attributes. Something cliché that would flatter her. My first glimpse of her not being like other women was when she didn't fawn all over the name or try to make more of it than what it was. If I'd known them what I knew now, I'd've named her my haven. In the few hours since she'd walked in the door, she'd allowed me to let my guard down in a way that I could only do around my parents. And even then it was limited because I always felt the weight of their expectations on my back.

A peace that was so easy for some to obtain was foreign to me. I couldn't let my guard down even when I was alone at night because responsibility plagued me at every hour of the day. My dreams were often filled with business deals and new ideas to streamline the processes of each of my investments to ensure I stayed on top. It wasn't greed or the love of money that drove my desire to maintain my level of wealth. It was the good that I was doing and could do more of as long as I was in the position I was in. The chronic over thinking, the intricate weaving and blending of my life amongst the others of this echelon of wealth in order to hasten the supposed *trickle-down effect* that never seemed to come to fruition. I was the keeper of many secrets only to reveal them when I needed an advantage. That was the weight that this woman, with her innocent smiles and lush curves, had unburdened from my shoulders in the matter of a few hours. I could only imagine what kind of magic she possessed between her thighs and what type of highs experiencing the warmth of her body would bring me.

As I kissed her, I felt like I couldn't get enough of her taste. As much as her presence gave me peace, her body felt so right underneath my fingertips, her taste was now a new addiction. I felt myself becoming more aggressive with each swipe of my tongue inside her mouth. Her moans did nothing but fuel the need I had to completely release the control I'd fought my entire adult life to maintain. To allow myself to just be instead of function within the confines of my image. But even now with all of this set up to get me to relax I just couldn't. Not that I wasn't falling into the fantasy of the moment. I was probably falling too quickly and too easily into step with the sanctuary we had created when we agreed to leave our lives at the door and indulge in one another. And that lost of power, because I had in effect given it to her, was causing me to fight against completely letting go.

In an attempt to keep things well organized I wanted to get inside her body as quickly as possible. My hands moved up from her ass and lifted up the hem of her shirt as they traveled upward. I gave her lips a break long enough to pull her shirt off and toss it somewhere in the room. Her skirt had been rucked up to her waist but now I wanted it off. The desire to control the situation was fading; outpaced by the raw desire her presence evoked. Something about her forced me out of the rigid constraints that kept my life the well-oiled machine that enabled me to exceed my goals. She made me desire her by simply being. And I no longer wanted to fight the urges that I had to let go. No matter what the consequences could be.

Heaven

I knew this was what I signed up for but a part of me thought I'd be far more reticent to just jump right into this feet first with no parachute.

But here I was happily doing this ho shit just as pleased as punch with myself. I feel like I was living the real life version of that Tweet song "Oops (Oh My)". My shirt had long since been dragged over my head leaving the black and red bra I'd purchased especially for this occasion exposed. At some point my skirt was slithered down my thighs after being bunched up around my waist as Adonis' hands took their time caressing me from my ankles to the tops of my thighs. His touch was more than electric. It was life giving. Sending not only pulses but revitalization into each and every part of my body that he came in contact with. My soul seemed to come out of the hibernation that heartbreak had forced it to enter and was urging me to receive the full benefit of all Adonis had to offer.

"Should we move this to the bedroom?" His words were mumbled somewhere in the vicinity of my left nipple and floated toward my ear as his lips encased it and his tongue teased it to the point of near pain. It was torturously hardened, extra sensitive, and had me on the verge of losing my mind. I was always so unsure of myself in the bedroom but something about Adonis made me want to throw that caution to the wind and take control. The anonymity of this situation gave me courage that many found in bottles or drugs but he was the only high I needed. I hoped that he would take me higher before the night was over.

With my hands on his lapels I pulled him from his feasting and his lips detached from my nipple with a pop.

"What's wrong with where we are right now?" My lips met his and began to apply the kind of pressure I hoped would incite him to give me what I wanted now instead of this slow teasing he was insistent upon performing.

He broke the kiss and looked at me curiously. Not like he was examining me but like he was confused at my words. "I would think —"

I smirked as I pressed my body even closer to his. I drew his ear toward my mouth before I took the lobe in my mouth and sucked on it. Allowing my teeth to gently scrape the sensitive skin I soothed any potential sting with my tongue. "And that's the problem," my words were breathy as I spoke directly into his ear.

I could hear him swallow as his hands continued to grip my ass keeping our bodies tightly joined. "And what is that?"

"The fact that after all of this you're still thinking and not just doing. Let me help you with that." I had worked his belt open as I'd spoken.

Luckily for me I was familiar with the *Hippique* belt buckle having played around with it at Hermès a few weeks ago. He made no move to halt my movements as I divested him of the clothing that covered his lower body. I sank into a squat and gathered my courage as I was met with what he was working with face to…dick.

Between porn, unsolicited dick pics while dating, and my own limited upclose experience I wasn't unfamiliar with the male anatomy. But like his name suggested I shouldn't have expected Adonis to have a run-of-the-mill dick. The shit was pretty. And dicks by nature are probably the ugliest thing to come out of God's seven day creating life binge but leave it to Adonis to break the mold. Seeing it up close let me know his shit had only been moderately hard the entire time he'd been feeling me up. As I stared, it continued to grow before my eyes. His length continued to take me by surprise but it was his girth that was shocking. It had to be pushing a diameter of five inches and a circumference of almost twice that. I hesitated before I glanced up at him. The arrogant smirk on his face riled my inner competitor and without further hesitation I forced my throat to relax and let this baseball bat he called a dick hit me in the tonsils.

"Fuck!"

I should've been proud of the way he'd shouted and how his entire body went rigid as I began to work him over. Some women couldn't stand the thought of giving head. I used to be one of them. It mainly felt like a chore. But watching this man whose power and self-assuredness seemed like a birthright near crumble as I French-kissed his sack made me feel as though I was the one who was powerful. The one who could and was controlling each aspect of this. The one who could make him weak in the knees.

As my tongue learned the exploratory and intimate knowledge of his dick, I knew it was special. Not only was it thick enough to rupture something within me, but it was veiny. Adonis had the kind of veins that crisscrossed, elevated, and flattened along his dick in a way that seemed especially crafted to hit every potential spot that one of his partners might have. And in addition to that, it had a downward curve. My mouth began to salivate even harder at thinking of how well it would hit the bundle of nerves behind my clit with each downward stroke as he pummeled my core from behind.

His hand went to the back of my head and for a moment I was self-conscious about this damned *hairmet* I'd allowed Sasha to convince me to wear. But remembering that I had no reason to feel any sort of way if that shit flew off I stopped giving a fuck and fully focused on the task at hand.

I became even more aroused as his hips began to thrust forward and his hand gripped the strands glued to my head. With a glance upward I could see how his eyes were attempting to stay trained on me but would flutter closed with each stroke of my tongue and collapsing of my cheeks.

I had been on some no hands shit since I started but I wanted to get him right so that this first encounter between the two of us was memorable. The last thing I needed was for him to get off after fifteen minutes of head and leave me unsatisfied. I ain't about to waste a body on whack dick so I needed to ensure he could bounce back after one orgasm. Getting this first nut out of the way would ensure he would last longer than minute. At least I hoped.

My hands met at the base of his dick as his hips continued to thrust. He seemed completely okay with getting his first nut out of the way and I was more than happy to oblige. I was only momentarily stunned again at the thickness of him. Had I not had a mouth full of dick I would've swallowed from nervousness. Instead I took him as deeply as possible using my hands to jack the rest of what I couldn't swallow as I began to work my throat around his head.

"Got damn girl…the fuck…?" I wanted to laugh but decided to hum on him in order to heighten his pleasure. My fucking jaws felt like they were about to dislocate from being stretched around him. "Heaven… swallow this shit for me…baby. I'm 'bout to—"

He didn't even get to finish his sentence before I felt his cum hitting every available wall of my mouth as he continued to thrust. I wasn't dumb enough to try and swallow that shit while he was thrusting that mammoth in my throat. He wasn't being disrespectful in his actions but that shit was just disrespectful in size naturally. When he finally stopped thrusting he looked down at me and let his dick fall out my mouth.

"Let me see it." I had to look a mess. My damn eyes had started to water and my chin was a mixture of all of our fluids but I did as directed and held my tongue out for his inspection. "Swallow it for me."

I did as directed and thought I was going to get a break so that he could regroup for round two but his dick hit me in the face before his cum was fully down my throat.

I'd read about this shit before but had never seen a nigga stay hard after he came.

My eyes drifted up to his and he was unbuttoning his shirt. His hand went to his solid gold cufflinks and by the time I met his eyes he was smirking down at me.

"I ain't never have a woman suck my dick like she owns that muthafucka. But if you thought I was going to tap out after some sloppy, you grossly underestimated the type of man you've got."

Since my mouth was empty I was free to gulp because a bitch was truly worried. And intimidated. His shirt fell to the floor and his cufflinks were tossed on top. I was graced with the view of the colorful ink that covered him from wrist to shoulder on both arms and across his entire chest. It stood in stark contrast to the gold of his skin and the nature of the man before me. I would have never thought underneath all that formality was—this.

He stood proudly before me in all of his naked glory and shit, if I looked like him I would too. He was lean and muscular reminding me of the guy who played Bruce Leroy in The Last Dragon.

His eyes roamed my body and with each spot his eyes caressed I felt my skin heat. *Pull it together, bitch. Confident and controlled.*

My natural reaction was to shy away from what I had done. Hang my head in shame at the way I'd let loose on him but I refused to be the regular Nev with him. I was Heaven tonight and I owned the role and moniker he'd bestowed upon me.

"By the time I get in that bedroom, I need you waiting on me. Face down, ass up with a smile and in them heels on you sashayed your pretty ass in here with earlier. Can you do that for me, Heaven?"

His hand once again found its place against the side of my neck and my eyes closed as I became intoxicated with the masculine energy that radiated off of him. Maybe that was what had me so drawn to him. It wasn't just his looks it was what he gave off. His presence and his aura were so commanding it was like he demanded respect before he opened his mouth. His lips grazed the spot beneath my jaw and I felt my body near seize from the simple pleasure. "Can you, Heaven?"

"Can I?" My mind seemed to short circuit the minute he touched me.

He pulled back and tipped my chin upward toward him. "Face down. Ass up. Those heels."

"Yes, sir."

CHAPTER FIVE

Hour Seven

Adonis

Quicksand.

That was what her pussy was like. Quicksand. If quicksand had a wet, silky texture that I could feel even through protection, then yep, quicksand. Her body seemed to suction me in like a siren luring men out from the sea to their deaths upon the rocks, only instead of staying dead I was held in her depths and allowed to be reincarnated with each pleasurable stroke I delivered and every contraction of her walls as she came.

When she attempted to end my existence by giving me the best head of my life and caused every system in my body to momentary shut down, I had to get her back. Not in a prideful way but because she'd earned that shit. Throughout all of this she had come in with the type of attitude that would've made me believe this wasn't her first time doing this. But her behavior at times gave away her novice status. For her to deep throat my dick without reservation had my mind gone. And I had to return the favor.

She'd done exactly what I'd wanted her to and dropped each article of clothing from the door of the bedroom over to the bed. She'd put an arch in her back so deep I swore she had some reptilian DNA because no human should be able to execute a curve in their spine like that. I'd stood there admiring the view for so long she had the nerve to look over her shoulder and ask *"what are you waiting for?"*

Wrong thing to say, li'l mama. I punished that tight ass pussy she had between her legs for all that mouth she had. The good ass mouth that had me wanting to whimper like a bitch and the sassy mouth trying to rush me when all I wanted to do was take my time and please her. She'd fucked that up and my ass lost damn near all control when I slipped inside those walls between her thighs. My man curved to her anatomy and I knew from the first thrust I was tapping on her spot. Three strokes in she started to wet my shit up and despite how much she covered my dick I could still feel every millimeter of her. She gripped me tightly and damn near held my dick hostage each time I plunged within her depths.

Her shit was magical which was only proven because I was laying here cuddling with her instead of doing everything I could to reclaim my personal space.

"Why did you agree to come and meet me tonight?" My fingers found themselves running along the outer curve of her breast as she nestled her body to me.

The question seemed to flow naturally after what just transpired but I couldn't help but be somewhat reserved because of the intensity of what I felt. The mind was a powerful thing and I wanted to be convinced that this was all in my head. The desire, the connection, how her simply being in my presence made my world slow down to a pace where I could enjoy being alive. It had to be all in my head, right?

"Are we being personal now?" I could feel her face pull into a smile against my chest and although we were close to crossing a line and divulging personal information about one another, I couldn't help but want to learn something. This felt all too real to me, and if this was the experience that Chuck and his staff were going to provide to other men like me, I had to get in on investing in this shit. I felt pride in the husky tone her voice had taken on. It was raspier than before, an ode to the heights of passion she'd been unable to camouflage that had been expressed with moans. Each word she spoke was a stroke to my ego.

"Only if you want to be." My fingers continued to caress her skin making the soft circles along her spine that I knew had to be relaxing her. She had long since dropped her guard and allowed herself to just be in the moment. Now I wanted her to connect with me in a small way, even if it was just for tonight.

The feeling of her breath on my chest and the resounding echo from the contact was the only whisper of sound in the room. An imaginary clock ticking inside my head counted off the seconds that passed before she spoke.

"I was supposed to be getting married today."

That was the last thing I thought she would've revealed.

The feelings of possessiveness and joy at her failed union shouldn't have flared up at the thought of her loss, but they did. And I wasn't going to delve into what more that could mean. Instead I tried to lighten the mood because her voice sounded somewhat somber. My arms shifted her body closer to mine on the Egyptian cotton sheets.

"You got cold feet?"

She chuckled and shook her head against my chest slightly. "Not me. He needed to find himself because he said I was far too set in *'who I was and what I wanted to accomplish'*."

Ah. So he fed her a crock of shit instead of dealing with his own inadequacies. "So he felt intimidated by your success is what you're saying." We had long since moved past getting personal and had delved into some shit that was akin to soul sharing.

"How do you know I'm successful?" The question was asked with a hint of humor but laden with the small uncertainty that tinted everything she'd said about herself that I found attractive. It was almost like a reflex of hers, the need to be constantly assured of someone's sincerity. If I hadn't already peeped that someone had beat that insecurity into her and the right man could take it away, I would've been aggravated. It made me wonder if the shithead she was supposed to marry had made her so insecure.

"Certain things I noticed. The way that you dress. Not draped in labels but in clothes that are beautiful and high quality. That is a sign of a woman that knows her mind and isn't afraid to be who she is. And your shoes kinda give it away."

I was sure that comment had her puzzled but she didn't ask the question I was sure was burning the tip of her tongue. "Continue."

My fingers continued to map a trail on the planes of her body as I simply enjoyed being with her. The post-sex sheen that covered her skin combined with the softness of her flesh. "Your clothes are classic, but your shoes have a seductive vibe of someone who doesn't need the approval of others. It sounds like you were too strong for your dude. Best to know that now, right?"

My eyes were glued to the figure that found some measure of comfort in my embrace and I watched her silent contemplation of my words. They weren't meant to offend, but they were meant to make her realize that whoever he was, he'd done her a favor. And a part of me didn't want her backtracking to bullshit.

"You're right." The breath she expelled ticked my exposed skin beneath her nose. "I hate to be a bother, but I'm starting to stick together, you mind if I wash off?"

"Not as long as you let me join you."

* * *

******

Once the bath was filled and was at max capacity with both bubbles, water, and humans, we both released a sigh as the warm water cushioned us. I was at one end of the claw foot tub and she was at the other holding the chrome sprayer that was affixed to the side. The matched the rest of the suite. The floors were black and white tile and the countertops were black stone with stark white cabinets. White towels were displayed on gold fixtures and the walls were covered in subway tiles. In addition to the immaculate black and gold clawfoot tub we were in, there was a huge shower on the other end of the suite near the water closet. I'd turned down the lights in keeping with the theme of romance.

"Tell me your greatest fear?" I was so enraptured with the sight before me I barely registered that she'd spoken. Her large breasts were two dark toffee mounds of perfection but wet with suds skiing down the slopes made them all the more erotic. My palms flexed as I kept the need to reach out and grab her to myself.

Shaking myself from the adolescent stupor I'd fallen in while ogling her form my gaze traveled up to her face. A face that held a look of extreme pleasure at my perusal instead of disdain at being visually molested. *Interesting.*

"Beg your pardon?"

She giggled and tossed a handful of suds in my direction. "Come on Adonis, this isn't a proper tea. *Begging my pardon* is a bit much for a post-coitus bath don't you think?"

"Slipped out." My eyes stayed focused on her face loving how at ease she was. I knew the point of the night was for us to get to this point but I was still somewhat surprised at how easily we seemed to go with the flow of it all.

"Then I still haven't made you as relaxed as I had hoped."

My fingers continued to do their best to memorize each inch of her flesh since I couldn't seem to keep my hands off of her. Hearing her words a smile played across my face. "Are you conceding failure?"

"No, simply analyzing the ways in which I may have fallen short now so that I can ensure victory later."

Her eyes weren't just glazed with lust, they were tinged with something almost...wild. Abandon maybe. Being fully committed to this moment and this time with me so that none of it went to waste. I could get down with that and apparently I needed to because I hadn't fully relaxed. Well that was a lie, I had, but then I slipped inside her and instead of only finding ecstasy between her walls her haven with its vise-like grip and texture of warm pancake batter offered me something more. Something I hadn't put a name on yet because that would make it too real. And I didn't have time for real. At least not past tonight.

The last thing I could do was get attached. But it was clear that Heaven was someone who could make anyone want to stay around her. *Proof positive that she was dealing with a clown before me.*

"To answer your question, my greatest fear is failure. Which is why I do everything in my power to be successful as often as I can. Now it's my turn. How smart are you?"

One of her beautifully smooth feet was now within my grasp and I began to knead the ball of her foot between my hands. Everything about her was unique. Whereas most men wanted a woman with a feet that were far too small for her frame, hers were larger than what some would deem dainty, connected to trim ankles and a firm calf. They were smooth, well cared for, and polished. Attractive despite what current society dictated they should be. Somewhat like the woman that was connected to them.

"What do you want? A full revealing of my education from grade school through college?" She didn't stiffen up at my inquisition but kept a playful smile on her face.

"I observe things," I kept my fingers easing into her flesh, "and I can hear that you try at times to keep how intelligent you are buried. You try and keep your phrases purely American but because of how much I've traveled I recognize that some of the phrases you use are from abroad. And then there's your speech. It has an underlying tone to it that I can't place but I know it's not from any part of the United States."

She didn't try to remove her foot but her face was far tighter than it should have been considering the way I know I put it down. The bath nor the massage were going to be enough to ease her mind again. Despite the fantasy we had created I couldn't help but observe what I'd revealed to her. There were other things but I felt like speaking about them would have her walking out of the room and I wasn't ready for her to leave. Another warning sign I should've probably heeded.

"I'm fairly intelligent. I wouldn't be able to afford to even glimpse at something like this if I wasn't." Her words were spoken in a way that let me know I'd put her on the defense. As if her bluster was covering up something that she didn't want me to know. So of course I had to ask.

"And how did a woman like you run across a service like this?"

"The same way as you did I would imagine."

She must negotiate a lot in her line of work because her ability to deflect rivaled my own.

"Mine happened by luck if I'm being real. And your face isn't one that I recognize so I'm sure we haven't run in the same circle before on any of the continents. Don't take offense to my words, but I know that although you have money, you're not the typical person they would approach to be involved in something like this."

"Well, if that didn't prove that you're a complete asshole I don't know what would."

"I meant no offense, love. But you have to understand that many people do what they need to in order to get next to me."

"And yet you had no worries about my motives when your dick was down my throat."

She attempted to hop out of the tub but I kept a firm grip on her foot. She eyed me with those windows that had only been filled with pleasure only a few minutes ago but were now harboring disdain and regret. Unabashedly I couldn't help but admire the view before me as the bubbles traipsed down her skin in an attempt to return to the water I hadn't bothered to remove myself from. No matter how short our time I didn't do that run away instead of talking it out bullshit. She was mine and needed to learn there were better ways to get over our differences. Especially when we'd had a miscommunication as small as this one.

"Let me go."

"You took what I said completely out of context. Do you think I think you're a prostitute? Initially I had that reaction because let's face it, you're far more beautiful than any of the women I've ever come across in my immediate circle. But as the night progressed I could tell that you're not some crazy stalker that's attempting to trap me for one of my kids. My people know who you are so if there was ever anything about you that I needed to handle I would do so. But I have taken great pains to come into this night with an open mind. I didn't expose your information to anyone or read it for myself. It was actually a compliment I was paying you saying that you're different. The women

I normally meet are those who frankly disgust me. They all have an angle. I like the anonymity that I have with you because I can be free. Let me ask you something." I released her foot because she probably needed it to balance and she slowly lowered it to the floor without attempting to leave.

"Do you know who I am?"

Her face frowned up and her lack of recognition of and annoyance was displayed. "Should I?"

"And that is why we are still here. You could've searched me out like I did you, but it's obvious someone that you trust gave you the green light to walk through the door. I won't press to ask who it was but the simple fact that you haven't played coy about knowing me or attempted to gather any type of information knowing that we have limited time with one another reinforces the fact that you're genuine. As much as you need to be desired, I needed to ensure you were as wholesome as you appeared to be. Imagine my surprise when you were. I make it a point to know everyone that is anywhere near my social stratosphere to avoid them. That is why I said what I said."

She visibly relaxed when I explained my words to her but I could tell she still had something on her chest.

"How do you know that I am not simply someone who refuses to be in the public eye?"

"Then we would be far more alike than I previously thought." In recent years I'd basically become a ghost, moving in silence out of necessity. Previously, I'd still been discreet about who I dealt with and my entire group of friends abhorred anything that had to do with the spotlight. If I was caught on camera or someone wanted to publish my likeness they quickly changed their minds. It was amazing how you could hide in plain sight so I knew she had no idea who I was.

"*Je suis profondément désolé.*" Her apology in French gave me additional insight into her upbringing and her stubbornness. She thought I'd missed her speaking Mossi earlier but I'd chosen not to bring it up. I observed and retained everything around me. An annoyance in my younger years that had my mother worried I was on the spectrum that had proven to be my greatest asset in adulthood.

"*Il n'est pas nécessaire de s'excuser.*" Her eyes widened slightly hearing me tell her there was no need to apologize. "Can we continue on with our night without issue or has my faux pas caused a rift?"

"We can continue but you probably need to get out of that tub. Your nuts are probably the size of raisins by now."

"I'd go through it again if it meant I got to see you like this."

"Like what?" That genuine curiosity was once again displayed on her face. That was what had me so enthralled with her. The authenticity of her emotions and the lack of hesitancy to reveal them to me. There was no strategy when it came to our interactions. But whose to say it wouldn't change if we had met under different circumstances?

"You truly don't understand how sexy you are, do you?" It was shocking to me. Too often women in my immediate vicinity were always trying to play up their sex appeal. Few tried the intelligent approach but it was always tinged with some type of sexual gratification: either the offer of it to get ahead or the expectation of mutual pleasure to gain a stronger foothold into my life or business. There were even a few who'd gone the innocent route before in an attempt to be different from the rest. But I knew that wasn't Heaven's angle. The small ways she tried to hide parts of herself from me that she thought weren't perfect. The looks of disbelief when I paid her a compliment made me wonder where she lived because all of the men that surrounded her had to be deaf, dumb, or both.

With that thought in mind I jumped out of the tub not caring about my dick swinging. I grabbed the towel that she was trying to use to cover herself up with and flung it onto the floor.

I knew she was becoming more comfortable with me when she didn't look alarmed by my slightly aggressive actions. She stood there and observed what I was doing in an almost scholarly way and it gave me an idea. She said she needed to be desired so I was going to force her to desire herself over anyone else.

I wrapped my arms around her and turned her to face the mirror that extended the length of the wall by the tub.

It was my turn to fall to my knees the way she'd done me. She took her eyes off the mirror which earned her a slap on her ass. Watching the way her flesh bounced at the contact had me more aroused. I repeated the motion this time with more exuberance and was rewarded for my efforts when a moan slipped past her lips.

"Spread them legs."

Without question she widened her stance and I watched her watching me from the mirror. She learned quickly but part of me wanted her to be disobedient so I could spank her ass again.

Maybe later.

I had a point to prove to her. She was truly oblivious to the power that she carried within her. I could read people well and Heaven was used to dimming herself so that others could shine. I couldn't tolerate shit like that and I wanted her to be at her full potential. And right now I was going to do it by making her cum.

"Adonis...I don't know—"

I leaned up and grabbed the towel from the side of the tub. No matter how many stars this hotel had I wasn't sitting my naked ass on a floor where dozens of other people had been. I went to my knees and simply looked at her pussy. I wanted her to feel uncomfortable or at least tense with anticipation, so I kept my hands to myself. What I saw had to be the prettiest set of lips I'd ever seen between a woman's thighs. They were a shade or two darker than the rest of her skin and they were juicy. There wasn't a bump in sight which let me know she got waxed on the regular. I couldn't stop myself from running my finger up the slit to test her wetness. Just like I thought, she might have been uncomfortable but she was simultaneously aroused.

"You already wet for me, Heaven? I ain't even taste you yet, baby." Her only response was a moan and for her deepen the arch in her back. "Put your leg on my shoulder, love."

She did as requested and I palmed her ass with my hands. I glanced up and she was watching me through the mirror with her bottom lip tucked between her teeth. Keeping my eyes on her face I extended my tongue and buried it between her lips. Her eyes immediately closed and her head fell back. I wanted her to watch me as I pleased her and I for damn sure wanted to see what she liked and didn't like. I kneaded the flesh of her ass again before I slapped it for her not following my direction.

"Eyes on the mirror."

She half growled half moaned as I continued to flick my tongue over her clit before using it to tunnel deeper within her walls. Her head came forward and she watched me make love to her with my tongue.

"Fuck...that feels...don't —" Her fingertips looked like they were about to scrap the glass and I wanted to laugh but I felt her walls start to squeeze the fuck out of my tongue.

"Feed me, Heaven." I replaced my tongue with two fingers then added a third when I felt how tight she still was. Women bragged about having snapback stomachs after birth but Heaven had that snapback pussy. She could take a dick like mine and shrink right back down to size afterward. I was immediately envious of the next man that would know the bliss of this hidden part of her and I took my frustrations out on her. My fingers began to rhythmically thrust, flutter and twirl within her as my lips found her pearl and began to nip and suck until she released the orgasm she'd been trying to fight all over my face.

"Oh...My...God!"

The leg that had been over my shoulder was now limply dangling. Her body began to slump toward the mirror and I used my hands to steady her keeping her center close to my face. I loved the taste and smell of her and I immediately craved her next release. Since I was never one to deny myself anything I began to lap at her folds again.

She immediately squeezed her thighs and tried to work her way away from me.

"Don't run away now, love. I'm not finished yet."

"Just leave me here to die in bliss." Her barely audible words forced a self-satisfied smirk to grace my face as she collapsed against the mirror.

"You want to get in the shower and clean up or can I coax you into the bedroom to sit on my face?"

She barely opened her eyes but the look on her face announced her surprise. "Sit on your face?"

"Did you think I was done? I really got to show you who the fuck you're dealing with, Heaven."

CHAPTER SIX

Hour Ten

Heaven

"Did you bring me out here for the view?"

The skyline of downtown Atlanta stretched before me in a cacophony of muted sounds and brilliant lights. The hotel must have held the air rights to several of the buildings surrounding it, because nothing was as high up as this penthouse suite for several blocks. When I asked he said that this area was called Buckhead and I knew for a fact it was where the uppity people lived.

Might need to scout a location here.

The view was beautiful and the air was cool enough to calm the warmth that still lingered after the way he'd fucked me like he hated me a few hours ago. And damn if I didn't love it. *Learn something new about yourself when you're fucking a stranger huh, Nev?*

I'd finally recovered from the literal tongue lashing he'd given me. Three back to back rounds of riding his face forced me to tap out for a nap. It was short lived because he woke me up with a platter of food, a new bottle of wine, and a request for me to meet him outside. It was after three in the morning but I wanted to make the most of what time we had left.

"You act like it's not spectacular." He was still behind me and when I turned he'd made himself comfortable on one of the outdoor couches. He'd flipped a switch and the outdoor heaters were now blazing. I was standing outside of the perimeter of their warmth because I could still feel the breeze that blew through the balcony. The wealth and sophistication that he surrounded him when I first laid eyes on him seemed to slightly lessened. It could be attributed to the change in his clothing and his demeanor. As soon as he began to shed the layers that were the outward hallmarks of his wealth, he was less rigid. Less controlled. Probably more of the him that he didn't let many people see. Even though I wasn't certain if it was fact, I was grateful for the potential of having witnessed him in his natural state of being. The anonymity made us both feel free.

I looked at him with a smile and crossed my bare legs as I leaned against the railing. I was clad in only a shirt, his, and the long sleeves protected my arms but nothing else. The wine was opened in front of him along with the food and the wine glasses but I couldn't help but keep my eyes focused on him. My heart danced at the sight of him and I wanted to take my fill while I could.

"It is, but it's not the scenery that is currently holding my attention."

"Oh really." The subtle shift in his hips was the only indication that my words had any effect. He had an amazing poker face and I swore once I stepped into my next life I was going to emulate this golden Adonis of a man whenever I needed to negotiate a contract.

"Let's go inside so I can show you." I felt emboldened by our anonymity, my desire for him, and my need to feel him again. He was, in a nutshell, the type of immediate gratification and ego stroke I needed. Whoever was the owner of this shit had a goldmine he was sitting on and didn't even know it.

At least it means Tee has job security.

"Why inside?" His eyes roamed over me lustfully and I preened beneath his gaze. Something that with any other stranger that would feel sordid was now, in a few short hours, a place of comfort where my mind and body could rest easy in the desire of his affections. In recent months that lustful gaze from the one I should've desired it from had become a place of revulsion and on some days, fear.

"Someone might see us out here." I might have been able to let loose when we were in the confines of a room but being outside where anyone from the neighboring buildings or flying above could see us wasn't something I could do. Could I?

"I thought you wanted to release your inhibitions? What better way to do it than out here?" He motioned around us with his hand and I took in the skyline again. There was a lot of activity but no one that could see us was focused on us.

"Well…"

"This ain't quite a patio, but 112 said it best, *we can do it anywhere*. Of course the idea of you in a shower soaking wet sounds pretty fucking enticing right now. Especially since I didn't get to feel that pussy in the bathtub." Another hip shift was accompanied by his legs spreading wider and his eyebrow quirking. "Isn't this what tonight is about,

Heaven? Exploring one another, letting go of whatever normally weighs us down? For me, it's image and expectations. What is it for you?"

"The feeling of being inadequate." I'd spoken that without hesitation even though I should've probably given more thought to my response. Not that what I said wasn't accurate. In fact, it was too accurate. Too spot on and way too revealing because I knew he would ask a follow up question. And I wasn't sure if I wanted to delve deeper into my psyche at the moment.

"In what way?" He eased himself further down in the sofa taking full advantage of its comfort. His posture had relaxed over the last few hours and the rigid almost militaristic form was replaced with his natural, less intense, carriage.

My arms wanted to fold across my chest defensively but I refrained because Adonis hadn't done anything wrong. "I told you, feeling desired."

He sat forward and braced his hands on his knees. Even in the early morning hour his skin seemed to reflect what little light that came from the buildings around us.

"I think it's more than that, something that hits you at your core. Makes you feel like you have to fight against the person or persons that made you feel undesirable in whatever area of your life. Fight against the way they tried to hold you back or hold you down. I'm more than happy to be the vessel in which you release your aggression. We are supposed to be here for each other, you took my aggression earlier without an ounce of fear, let me take yours in kind."

As he spoke I'd been slowly walking toward him almost hypnotized by the way he'd spoken to me, saw through me, and touched a part of me I hadn't wanted to be brought to light yet. Hadn't been ready to deal with yet and wouldn't know where to begin if I tried. He was the charmer and I was the snake entranced by the melody he played to bring me closer into the web, the trap, and whatever confines awaited me I wanted to surrender to them. To unburden myself of the weight and transfer it to him.

"Take what you need."

Four words. Four words no one, no lover had ever spoken to me before that resonated to the depths of me none of them had ever reached. Let alone set out to find. But here he was, in a matter of hours, picking apart pieces of me as if he knew where they were hidden and had been trapped within my person until he along to uncover them.

Seeing I wasn't going to hesitate, he allowed me to do what I needed to. With a small lift of his hips he allowed the throbbing muscle I was more than happy to become reacquainted with to spring free. He sheathed his protruding scepter of desire and presented the throne for which he wanted me to rest my worries and I was more than happy to oblige.

A mutual moan was all that could be heard in the small space of time that we occupied. I started to sink onto him slowly and he kept my lips pinned to his by initiating a kiss that kept my face close to his rendering it immobile. My pubic, sacral, and lower extremities were the only parts of me that continued to move. My arms wrapped around his body as he kept his to his sides allowing me to take while he gave of himself.

I fully impaled myself on him feeling more and more lost and simultaneously found the deeper into me that he got. Once I was full, I began carefully rock against him with him inside of me almost afraid of doing what should have come naturally.

"Stop thinking, Heaven." The command was a breathy whisper against my lips as his poker face contorted into something slightly less controlled and leaning more on the side of beautifully tortured. The reaction of a man like him to me strengthened the parts of me he had already started to rebuild with his acceptance, fortifying my ability to be sexual without being in my head and worried.

This was overall something different than before. Before had been a beautiful relinquishment of my responsibilities and the weight of my problems. But this felt like him giving me permission to carry the burden because I now had the confidence that I could bear them without issue. That I was stronger than I'd given myself credit for. More than being the Future Mrs. of anyone. That being me was enough. There was nothing wrong with me like I'd led myself to believe for all these months.

When the first tear fell I felt his weight shift while he was still deeply embedded within me. Something had changed, a transference of some sort and I relinquished control over to him despite not knowing accurately what it was. When he stood, my legs wrapped around his muscular waist on their own volition and before I could utter the words in my head he requested my trust so I gave it.

With each step away from the warmth we began to create our own. Each stride forward was him hitting a new portion of my anatomy and discovering some hidden erogenous zone that hadn't previously existed before he was there. I felt the coolness of the metal and the increased sounds of life below and I knew I was on the railing.

My eyes met his and he silently asked for me to trust him and once again my agreement was given without reservation. If this was the way I was meant to die I for damn sure might embarrass a few people but I would have fun while doing it.

His hand snaked toward my neck as my head dangled over the side of the building. His fingers wrapped around the my throat and gentle pressure was applied as his other hand held me possessively and protectively against his frame. Each thrust was an exercise in duality: the danger of the situation only seemed to heighten the pleasure caused as each thrust made me increasingly aware of the predicament I could be in if one thing went wrong.

But the grasp he had on my body and his intense focus on keeping me safe while providing me with pleasure struck some twisted chord within me that I didn't know was there. The rush of blood to my head and the gentle pressure to my neck coalesced into some weird erotic asphyxiation that had me raining down another orgasm all over his dick.

"That's what I wanted to see. Wet my shit up, Heaven. Look at all that cum on my dick. I make you feel good, baby?"

I could hear every word he spoke but he sounded so far away. I could only nod my approval at the precise way he handled my body.

To show his appreciation for my cooperation and the submission of my body to his control Adonis leaned down and thrust his tongue into my mouth with the same fervor and rhythm as his dick pounded into my core. My legs were hiked up higher on his waist, my body eased up from the precipice of destruction and the hand that had been at the base of my throat was now wrapped around my waist gripping one ass cheek as he all but tried to break my pelvis.

"Fuck!" Sweat now mixed with tears as my body clung to his again allowing him to carry us. Gone were the reservations about this night, being outside, and about myself. I wanted to yell but it was caught in my throat. All of my energy was going into keeping myself from blacking out at the hurting he put on me. I would've never thought that he was so talented at first glance and now I was paying for misjudging him. Happily paying though.

He seemed to widen within me and I knew he was close to reaching his peak. We climaxed together on a gasp and I held him tightly within me. My body was sore from accommodating him and I knew tomorrow would be even worse. He kept my legs around his waist and made no move to remove his dick. It had gone down but not enough for it to slip out of me on its own.

He kept his dark brown eyes focused on mine as he seemed to be searching for something. "What are you doing to me, Heaven?"

I held his gaze allowing him to look as deeply into my soul as he wanted to. As I peered deeply into his eyes I could see the lust and the longing that he attempted to conceal within them.

"Exactly what you're doing to me."

******

We were now using the patio in the way it was intended. Of course I didn't see anything wrong with the way we'd christened it previously. My body melded into his as we sat on the sofa covered by a blanket he'd retrieved from the bedroom. The artificially warmed air provided an additional barrier to the colder temperatures that we were now experiencing. Funny how I didn't feel it when I was playing with my life. *Good dick is a hell of a drug.*

"I could get used to this."

My confession was whispered softly and I had hoped it had been muffled by the wind. But I'd been granted too many favors this night by way of good company and orgasms so my blunder wasn't hidden.

"I know exactly what you mean."

The stoic sound in his voice reminded me that he was cynical about all of this, hence the reason why he was here in the first place. I was looking for the safety and instant gratification of a fully vetted tryst whereas this was the only way he could imagine himself letting go. My heart skipped with agony for him momentarily because although what I had with my ex ended up being a lie, I'd at least been able to live in the fantasy for longer than one night. Thinking on it, I wasn't sure who was better off though, him who knew he could only have this for short bits of time or me who'd had it and realized none of it was real. Both seemed equally fucked up the more I thought about it.

"You remind me a bit of one of my associate's wives. She's got the kind of mind that makes you hang on every word she says. She walks into the room with confidence because she owned it before she even arrived." He got silent, his eyes still on the darkness of the horizon before he spoke again. "I always did admire that about her." The admiration in his voice gave me pause.

"Is that a weird way to say you're crushing on dude's wife or—"

"No, Heaven. It was meant to be a compliment to you. I thought that women like her who could be beautiful, intelligent and women of substance were unicorns. Now that I've met the both of you it really opens my eyes up to how worthless some of the people I come in contact with are."

I snuggled in closer to him and listened to his voice vibrate within his chest. "Maybe not worthless. Maybe they're just not meant to have any type of impact on your life and they're merely…superfluous."

"Expendable is probably the best word."

"If you say so, Adonis."

"I can't help but allow my chest to poke out a little bit further every time you call me that."

"Why?"

"Adonis was the god of beauty and desire. So you're basically saying I'm fine as hell and you want me. Coming from a woman like you that's some shit to be proud of."

Now my curiosity was piqued. "A woman like me?"

"Cultured, not for the sake of saying you are but actually having experienced other cultures for a deeper understanding of others. Intelligent because from what I gather you speak at least three languages and you have what I can assume is a keen mind for business. You're fucking gorgeous in this sexy ass, girl next door that I still want to do nasty shit to like eat her pussy from the back kind of way." I couldn't help but interrupt what he was saying with laughter because he'd completely relaxed and was saying whatever the hell came to his mind. "And you don't want anything from me but my time. And even though that's probably my most expensive commodity because of the person you are I'm more than happy to give it to you."

My laughter stopped because that felt…real. Heavy. Prophetic in a way. Like what he was going to want from me now was deeper than what he'd needed at the beginning of the night. Part of me wished I'd requested an entire weekend with him because one night wasn't going to be enough but it had to be. And besides, if I was finding it difficult to walk away after a night, I could only imagine what damage a weekend with him could do.

"Damn, I leave you speechless?" His chuckled rumbled through his chest beneath my ear and it caused me to smile again.

Discreetly I inhaled. "I mean, that was probably the sweetest thing anyone has ever said to me if I'm being honest."

He made a sarcastic sound between a grunt and a huff before he spoke. "Well that confirms it."

"Confirms what?"

"That you were fucking around with the wrong kinda nigga if the truth is the sweetest thing you've ever heard."

I buried my head further into his chest and I wasn't sure if I was attempting to hide my embarrassment or my glee at his words. His chest had quickly become my safe haven. When I molded my feminine softness against his muscular, masculine planes, we fit together perfectly. And that revelation was amongst the things that hurt. Not that we worked so well together but the cruel reality of finding someone that seemed to fit and I couldn't have him. Past all of the obligations of the arrangement we'd made with this service, Adonis had spoken many times of his inability to balance having it all. There was no room in his life for something as serious as I would want us to be. It went deeper than amazing sex. In the hours between hello and now, I couldn't help the feeling of déjà vu that kept smacking me in the face. Not in the sense that I'd met him before but the type of awarenesses that I knew this man intimately and completely in a past life and we were reuniting in this one to correct our wrongs. Only we'd apparently been dealt the wildest hand imaginable because any communication outside of the walls of this suite would result in legal action. *Why couldn't I meet his fine ass at a Starbucks like a normal woman?*

"You most definitely have a point in saying that."

"Took you long enough to agree with me." His voice was low but I could still hear his joking tone.

"I rarely speak without careful contemplation."

"Well damn, now I'm the one questioning if I put it down well enough if you're still over here thinking and shit."

"Have no fears, I'm sure the suites on the next block over know your name."

"Keep it a buck, your ass couldn't even speak so how would they know?"

My mouth hung open momentarily stunned before I nudged him in his shoulder playfully. "Shut the hell up!"

His laughter rang out before it tapered and a serious mien took over. "Naw but for real. It's getting late let's head inside."

"Your old ass getting tired on me, Adonis?"

The boastful smile that graced his face let me know I was in for some shit when we entered the suite.

"Who said shit about sleeping, Heaven?"

CHAPTER SEVEN

Final Hours

Adonis

"You never said why you were here." My body engulfed hers once again on the bed as I silently reveled in her presence. After the experience on the balcony, the depth of my need for her was far more intense than anything I'd experienced before. That give and take, the trust with her life literally in my hands, her body mine to command and to pleasure, was a heady encounter that I knew needed to be repeated far more often than what this service could provide.

In a few short hours this California King had become our sanctuary. These four walls, two black two white, had become the shelter from the outside world. We were snuggled deeply beneath a snow-white comforter that I was sure would need to be tossed after we got done with this room. I doubt a washing would get rid of the amount of fluids that we'd both left on it. The bed was the focal point and full on luxury with a gold leather tufted head and footboard and inlaid diamond accents.

That soft giggle infiltrated my ear from where her face was buried in the side of my neck. Her lips brushed against my skin as she laughed and I loved the delicate feel of her lips on my flesh. It was titillating and made all the more alluring by the innocence of it.

"I already told you that I what I was supposed to be doing on Valentine's Day this year."

"Yeah, but it doesn't tell me how you ended up here. That lends itself more to your and your girls getting up and going on the honeymoon you and ya nigga had planned without him. Not you laid up with me. So, tell me again my Heaven, why are you here?"

I kept my eyes focused on her body although I could feel her tilt her head up and look at me. "I thought we weren't supposed to cross those lines."

It was odd to me knowing how much had transpired between us, not just the sex but the connection I knew she'd felt, yet she was still asking these questions. I'd touched, tasted, and licked every portion of her body and I knew I'd penetrated her mentally so all of this mystery was unnecessary at this point. "Considering the things I just did to your body; I think we are pretty well enough acquainted for me to ask you that."

She giggled again and it felt like foreshadowing of how I would spend every night for the rest of my life. Lying in bed with this woman contemplating the what ifs and mapping out a future that was only as iridescent as it was because of her. "Is it trite if I say I'm too busy for anything real and I needed to scratch an itch?"

"Pretty expensive way to scratch an itch. You must be someone important."

"Not at all, I'm really a nobody. What about you, sir? What's your story? Why are you here with me tonight when I'd swear on my life that you're pretty perfect."

I shrugged my shoulders at her words because I was used to hearing people make that assumption about me. It was easier to reveal the truth to her in the comfortable confines of darkness. "This is the easiest way to have what I want that I know I can't have." The emotional weight of the words seemed to rest heavily in the air between the two of us.

She sat up then and stared me in the eyes. "And why can't you have it?" Her question was meant to garner the information she wanted but in a way that was non-threatening. She looked confused, as though she thought I was a man who could handle any and everything so what I was going to say had to be monumental.

"Because life isn't set up for you to get everything that you want." By the disappointment on her face I knew she thought I was just saying some shit to get her off the subject but that was honestly what it was. I couldn't be everything to everyone and honestly no one before made me think twice about the way I was moving. Not enough to slow down for and make them priority. Not until this woman with her mystery and temptation walked into my hotel room.

"Somehow I think you're the type of man to defy the odds if you really wanted to."

I felt it again. That tug for this to be more than what it was; a beautiful moment. Just a night of pleasure and the ability to let my mind go momentarily. The tug for there to be an exclusivity, a realness, to whatever it was this was.

"Give me something beautiful to remember you by. That way when I'm lonely I can remember this night and realize that just for tonight, I had everything I wanted all at once."

She leaned over and did the one thing we swore we wouldn't do. She looked deeply into my eyes, the dark brown of hers a near ocean of dimension against her medium brown skin. Her hand came up to the side of my face and caressed it gently with a tenderness I had never felt from a woman that wasn't my blood before. She leaned over and kissed my forehead first, with an adoration that made me close my eyes as if I could ward off the emotions she was attempting to draw forth. It was like those lips on my brain were attempting to withdraw my common sense and break down every wall of protection I'd built up to keep her and everyone else out.

Her lips swept over my nose next, her top and bottom lip carefully caressing the tip before moving south and hovering over mine. I was rigid with anticipation and wanting to feel her lips on mine. Each exhalation of her soft breaths against my face built up the desire and expectation of what was yet to come.

When she finally obliged my brain almost shut down. The heat that was caused by the reaction of my body to hers was far deeper and more potent than when my dick was thrusting in her depths no more than an hour ago.

This kiss was something that removed another layer of what I had blocking the wall around my emotions. She hadn't broken it down, but she was doing something to the foundation that made it far less stable than it had been before. This kiss was emotional. I felt the longing within her because it mirrored what was within me. The want for more. Of the life that everyone already assumed you lived because you'd painted this perfect picture for the masses because no one wanted to see your reality. She'd shared with me some of her pain, but I wanted to carry the remainder of her burdens.

I didn't want to deepen the kiss. I wanted it to be filled with this softness, gentleness, to savor it for the momentary escape from reality that it provided. I'd found heaven in her body the entire night, now I was finding solace, peace, in her kiss. A glimpse of what could be if I did more than I should have. Long days ending in nights recharging with her energy, immersing myself in the beauty of her spirit. Innocent vixen eyes smiling at me over the edge of a drink as we escaped from a family gathering to enjoy one of the carnal pleasures I'd come to enjoy so immensely with her. She'd be my rock, the one thing in my life that could hold me steady. I'd be her waters, the one thing that aided and soothed the transitional path she had to take into this next phase of life so that we could grow together into something beautiful. Magical.

"What is your name, my Heaven?" I looked into her eyes and she wore a dreamy expression that I was sure mirrored my own. Emotions crept to the surface whenever we interacted. The mutual need for the continuance of the deepening of what we started tonight.

She hesitated and it was almost as if the spell was broken in the realm we'd created within these two thousand square feet. Her eyes fell to my chest, unable to rise to meet mine and I didn't know if she was contemplating or thinking of a reason to let me down easily.

"I can't. And I want to explain to you why, but it could put someone in jeopardy and as much as I want to Adonis—"

"You can't." I didn't mean for it to sound as dry as it did, but my frustrations couldn't be masked. I couldn't help that I wanted the sparkle that I'd seen in her eyes to be there for me when I awakened in the morning. And each one after that. Something about her drew me closer to the edge of calling up Raph and making him snatch off the blinders of her identity.

But the simple fact that she wouldn't volunteer the information let me know I would forever allow it to stay hidden in the depths of my mind. Maybe in a year when I got tired of thinking of what could've been or should've been, when my friends' anniversary parties got to be too much for me or the birth of their children gave me too much of an ache I might look her up. But for right now I would leave it be. I never asked anyone for anything. I never allowed myself to be vulnerable enough to have to face their rejection. And her answer was reinforcing why I was the way I was. It stung for her to so cavalierly remind me that this was for one night and someone else's feelings were of a greater concern to my own. Could I be tripping since I'd known this woman for less than twelve hours? Probably. Call it selfishness or the need for me to have my way when I wanted it but I could've sworn that kismet had happened between us. Something that should've felt transcendent, an anomaly among the ordinary and yet she didn't put as much stock into it as I did. Which let me know I was probably overthinking this entire situation.

She looked near tearful as she saw me shut back down. I was no longer the person that had opened up to her for the last day. I was back to being me. No more laughter would be had. For the remaining few hours that were left in this rendezvous, I had to put back on the mask and shield my emotions. I'd be a liar if I didn't admit, even just to myself, that the part of me unmarred by a pile of cynicism and expectations was hurt at her inability to drop the pretenses.

There was no need to be angry at her. She was following the rules and it was me who was breaking them. The ones on paper and the unspoken ones of nature that seemed to try and drive me into some level of depth with this woman that was surely not attainable after such a short amount of time getting to know her. The mind was powerful and mine wasn't just good at business, it was obviously a master at deception and imagination. So good that it had tricked itself into believing in something that wasn't real, never had been, and probably never would be. But, in my loneliest moments I could fall back onto the memories of when I found love in one night.

****

I woke up to a cold side of the bed regretting that I didn't go with my first mind and try to find out more about her while she was here. Instead, we'd had a standoff for a few moments before I wrapped her up in my embrace and instructed my body to memorize the feeling of us being connected. Imprinting her into the depths of my subconscious so that when I needed a moment of solace I could retreat to the place in my head that held this night, these feelings and the emotions that had arisen from it all. For now, that had to be enough.

All I had was her face, one that I hadn't even bothered to capture on film to memorialize the moment of her being with me. Of there having been an *us* in any shape form or fashion. That was how caught up in the fantasy of her I was. The phone on the bedside table rang and I answered it knowing it was for me.

"Yes?"

"Sir, I wanted to remind you that our takeoff time is less than an hour away."

I sighed realizing how late I'd actually slept. Raph had a thing about my ass being on time and I could hear how annoyed he was. "My guest, did she leave safely?"

"Yes, and the gifts that you requested be purchased were slipped into her luggage on the way out." We'd gotten so caught up in one another that she'd never seen nor worn any of the items I'd purchased for her. And I felt not a twinge of disappointment.

"Where did she go?" I was reaching, hoping that he would let something slip even though I told his ass to deny me if I questioned him.

"We aren't sure. Once we escorted her out, she had an Uber pick her up. We can grab the license plate if you want—"

I remembered myself and the litany of obligations that I had on my shoulders. She was sweet, innocent and someone that I wouldn't want to draw int the world that I had one foot in and one foot out of. I was often called Batman, but in truth I was more Harvey Dent. I wore two faces with more ease than most people could wear one.

I could be as ruthless as a mafia don and as poised as a CEO, probably because I was basically both.

Knowing there was no use I gave my answer. "No, leave it alone."

Raph hesitated before he responded. "Gotcha, boss."

I got up and handled my hygiene as quickly as I could. And although I wanted to lie to myself, there was no way to deny that I wanted her scent to linger on me as long as possible, so I skipped a full shower. I checked the room to ensure I hadn't left anything when I saw an envelope with the words *My Adonis* written on the front. If I stopped and read the letter, I would turn this city upside down until I found her. Swallowing my selfish desires once again, I grabbed the inconspicuous overnight bag I'd used for the night, shoved the letter inside, and slung it over my shoulder before leaving the room.

Reaching the elevator I was joined by the two people trusted with my life daily. We were already on the penthouse level so I used the keycard to give us access to the roof.

"Takeoff is in fifteen minutes, boss."

My silent head nod was the only acknowledgement he would get from me. My mind was torn between last night and this morning. The man I wanted to be versus the one I really was. Just like I'd told her, there was no way for me to have it all. No matter what I wanted. And the last thing I wanted to do was give Raph's ass the satisfaction of being right. Even though he was. I was dressed up in a full suit as usual and he mirrored my formality although it was the weekend.

When we stepped off onto the roof, I was pleased to see my staff was already ready to go. I handed off my bag to the valet that was waiting by the door and took my coffee from the concierge. I walked over to the machine happy the that the blades weren't turning yet and I could still hear myself think.

"Have a safe flight, sir." The concierge was working extra hard this morning by coming up and greeting me and although I wanted to keep going, the CEO had to perform.

I reached out and shook his hand with a smile. "Thank you, the stay was exceptional as always."

He damn near beamed at me with how wide his smile was. "Delighted to hear that, sir."

With a smile that I could only muster up when I thought of her, I turned and walked toward the helicopter.

"Where are we headed?" The question was directed toward Raph as I began to buckle into my seat and prepare for takeoff.

"There are two meetings that you have today. Both are in Charlotte. The chopper will take us to the airport where your plane is already waiting."

I nodded my head and slipped the headset over my ears as the blades began to whirr in earnest. "Good. Schedule me for as much as you can, please. I have a lot on my mind."

He nodded and followed suit as two of my security team strapped in as well. "What did you think of the service? Something you want to buy into?"

I stopped my cup of coffee halfway to my mouth and looked at my assistant. "No."

Confusion peppered his face as he tucked his iPad beneath his leg. "No? You seemed to be gung-ho about it last night."

"I still am. I don't want to buy in, I want to own it. Look into that for me will you?"

He chuckled and did a checkmark symbol in the air with his finger. "Right away, sir."

I turned and looked at the intricate emblem on my helicopter interior and released a sigh. That logo represented me in more ways than one. The intertwined M and W it spoke to who the world saw, the gilded M and who I really was, the black W. Everything I did was for my last name, not my first. And sadly I'd just let the only woman I thought I could bestow it on walk out of my life without another word.

"We'll be landing at the airport in fifteen minutes Mr. Warren." The pilot made sure to let me know as we began to lift.

"Thank you, Vic."

As much as my vixen stayed on my mind she had to keep to the recesses. Anything other than that would mean I would be distracted, and one thing that Midas Warren didn't do with either one of his faces was fuck up.

As we lifted off the ground I left her there in the penthouse suite of the hotel that bore my name. In the early hours before the sun rose, I'd broken my rule and left a breadcrumb as to who I was. If it was meant to be, then she'd reach out. I couldn't and wouldn't distract myself with her letter. I'd already stepped out once and gotten rejected. If her letter was more of the same, I didn't want to know. Not now. For now, I'd have to be satisfied to have found a lifetime of love in one night and sadly, one night was all I was going to get.

The End….for now.

Power Within the Stars Series:

A Shift in the Stars

Ajabu.

* * *

In Swahili, it means wonder but, to those who inhabit this realm that mirrors Earth, it is the land of the ancestors, of gods and those who draw their strength from the stars. Over the millennia alliances have been drawn and changed, and now all that remains are three crucial areas of power: the West, the East, and the In-between.

The Eastlands are ruled by the powerful Mwanga-Kimani monarchy of lion shifters. They have kept to the ways of old and their land is prosperous because of their devotion. The crown prince Zorion Mwanga-Kimani has found his fated mate, Princess Isabis, ensuring the continued favor from the gods.

The In-between is where the primary protectors of the realm reside. They are currently led by the Kamau family and strive to live in harmony with nature but remain set apart from both kingdoms. Edgernon Kamau was dismissed from the Westland court decades ago, thus driving the separation. Rieka, daughter of Edgernon, is focused on living up to her parent's and her people's expectations.

The magic of the Westlands is dying. The ruling monarchy, the Odhiambo-Njeri, the wolf shifters, have strayed from the true mate prophecies and now their land is suffering. Further draining their resources and the light from their soil are the Others: a group of former residents of Ajabu who ventured to other realms and returned changed. The

King of the Westlands, Ozouf Odhiambo-Njeri, is desperate to find a way to restore magic to his land. Driven by his personal demons and held back by a queen he doesn't love, the king is sinking further into despair.

Dark forces are gathering in an attempt to overthrow the peace that has existed for centuries. The fate of Ajabu rests on the shoulders of these four warriors. Will they find the power to right their fates or will the magic of Ajabu be lost?

Rise of the Others

Ajabu is healing, but as Ozouf told his sek reyna, the battle had only begun.

Having found his mate and now expecting an heir, the magic has returned to the Westlands. But the king and his newly crowned queen are not able to rest and enjoy matrimony as they expected. Sybilla is plotting with a new enemy long thought dead and the consequences for this miscalculation are tragic.

The Eastlands have long since been the most prosperous area of Ajabu, but changes are coming. The child that Princess Isabis carries is unlike anything that Ajabu has seen in many millennia. A mistake on her part allowed him to be changed, but is that change for the better or the worse?

The gods are awaiting their moment to reclaim their home and aid their children in defeating their enemy. Will they be patient enough to put the proper pieces in place, or will the desire to act now ensure defeat before the war begins?

Dark forces are strengthening all around and new heroes and enemies arise to take their rightful place. Will the distractions thrown at them cause them to lose sight of the gods' plan or will they put aside their own desires for the fate of Ajabu?

Have you met the Orphans?
Orphan Series

Fortunate

I'm nobody's Cinderella.

* * *

Because I learned at a young age that fairytales aren't real, and there's no such thing as a Prince Charming waiting to save you, at least not for a girl like me. So, I learned to save myself and everyone else I loved. And I would've been satisfied with that life. Until he came along sprinkling fairy dust and offering to shoulder burdens I didn't even realize I was carrying. And now what am I supposed to do when he's offering me a life I never wanted, but one he thinks I deserve?

I'm nobody's Prince Charming.

Because in this life, I'm the dreaded F-word: famous. And when you're young, black and wealthy, you learn that people will use you for whatever they need and keep it moving. So, I kept my circle small until she swept me up in her chaos. And I happily went along with it just for the chance to make her mine. But how do you commit to someone who doesn't think she's worthy of being kept?

Asylum

* * *

What's in a name? That which we call a rose by any other name would smell as sweet. -William Shakespeare

Wilhelmina Briggs is a nobody. But Billy Briggs, the professional name she goes by, is a formidable opponent in the sports management world. As part of B and B Sports Management, she's kept the line between business and pleasure from being crossed. Until a blond bombshell in Berlutis captures her attention and refuses to let go. And causes her to wonder if the potential hit to her professional reputation is worth the risk.

Don't judge a book by its cover because looks can be deceiving – Lester Fuller and Edwin Rolfe

Jacoby Murdoch might look like the typical All-American man, but he's not. After enduring a childhood few would have survived, he made his way to the pinnacle of his career. Having little knowledge of what unconditional love is, it's not on his radar. Until he needs the allusive Billy Briggs and his partner to take his career to new heights. And he learns that he is a she and he can't deny the attraction. No matter how much she tries to keep it professional. But fate sets out trials, and as Jacoby's history is revealed he reaches new heights before his own arrogance and privilege threatens his relationships. While Jacoby is learning about the new parts of himself and his past, will it prevent him from securing the only woman he wants for his future?

What happens when the fairytale isn't all you thought it would be?

All that glitters ain't gold.

* * *

Boy meets girl. Boy loves girl. Girl loves boy back. Life should be perfect, right? Even when you get your fairytale, trouble can come at you from all angles to throw off your happily ever after. Ev, Billy, and Kat have all faced trials and tribulations that would have broken weaker women. Now, each woman is working through her own issues and learning to live within her new normal.

Being constantly thrust into the spotlight means having to watch out for those praying for your downfall. With secrets being kept on all sides, in the end, love may not be enough to restore trust

once it's broken.

Worthy

Friends. Then lovers. Then enemies. Now they're somewhere in between. The baggage is too heavy and they're both trying to release the burden. But is freedom what they really want?

Beauty knows pain.

Katherine Garner is the epitome of a survivor. No parents, friends turned family and tragedies that should have torn her apart. But she made it out with the battle scars to prove she's a fighter. Now at a crossroads, she has to determine if the life she always thought she wanted is truly who she is deep down inside.

Save the day, be the hero, get the girl.

Despite vowing to protect and serve and living his life by the rules, Malcolm still hasn't achieved everything in life he wants. But two out of the three ain't so bad. But try as he might Malcolm Williamson knows that despite all her shortcomings the love he has for Kat will never die. The tables have turned and she's no longer begging for his love. Will he miss out on his first and forever love by letting someone else take his place?

Past and present threats are colliding to try and rip these two apart permanently. Will they be able to trust each other enough to overcome those who wish to see them fall? Or will their inability to be honest be the reason they miss out on love and possibly lose their lives?

Made in the USA
Columbia, SC
16 September 2025